What was it about Bonnie that had bewitched him so?

It couldn't be just her physical beauty. She was lovely...yes....

No, it was something else, something...intangible. A vulnerability perhaps? The thought made him almost laugh. The coolly competent Mrs. Merrick vulnerable? The clever, conniving Mrs. Merrick...?

She was a witch, a sorceress, a caster of spells....

MIRANDA LEE is Australian, living near Sydney. Born and raised in the bush, she was boarding school educated and briefly pursued a classical music career before moving to Sydney and embracing the world of computers. Happily married, with three daughters, she began writing when family commitments kept her at home. She likes to create stories that are believable, modern, fast-paced and sexy. Her interests include reading meaty sagas, doing word puzzles, gambling and going to the movies.

Books by Miranda Lee

HARLEQUIN PRESENTS
1791—MISTRESS OF DECEPTION
1811—THE BRIDE IN BLUE

AFFAIRS TO REMEMBER

1849—A KISS TO REMEMBER
1855—A WEEKEND TO REMEMBER
1861—A WOMAN TO REMEMBER

1878—A DAUGHTER'S DILEMMA
1884—MADDIE'S LOVE-CHILD

Miranda LEE

A Haunting Obsession

A HAUNTING OBSESSION

Harlequin Books

**TORONTO • NEW YORK • LONDON
AMSTERDAM • PARIS • SYDNEY • HAMBURG
STOCKHOLM • ATHENS • TOKYO • MILAN
MADRID • WARSAW • BUDAPEST • AUCKLAND**

ISBN 0-373-11893-7

A HAUNTING OBSESSION

First North American Publication 1997.

Copyright © 1995 by Miranda Lee.

Printed in U.S.A.

CHAPTER ONE

JORDAN VINE-HALL sat at his large leather-topped desk, drumming the fingers of his right hand and glaring down at the phone. It had taken all of his control not to slam the damned thing down after speaking with that woman. Even now—several seconds later—his temper was still frayed around the edges.

Who did she think she was, treating him like that? Didn't she know the adage that the customer was always right? Any real-estate agent worth his or her salt would have been fawning all over him, not giving him the proverbial cold shoulder.

OK, so he'd been a bit brusque initially, and he'd probably piqued her undoubtedly feminist nature by saying he'd asked for a salesman. But so what? Her job was to sell him a house, not make snap judgements on his possible chauvinism. She should have hidden her irritation, not snootily told him that she was, in fact, a valued member of Coastal Properties' sales staff, but if he insisted she would pass him on to one of her male colleagues.

Perhaps he should have let her do just that!

Hell, he had a good mind not to go at all. Let her wait and sweat for nothing. No doubt, underneath, she thought she was on to a sure sale with his having said money was no object. Serve her right if he didn't turn up. God, she hadn't even had the decency to crawl a little once she'd known she had money on the line.

A wry but somewhat reluctant half-smile curved one corner of Jordan's normally serious mouth and he leant

back into the deep leather chair, elbows on the padded
arm-rests, his long fingers steepled in front of his chest.
He supposed he had to admire her for that. It was even
a pleasant change in a way. And rather intriguing. He
was used to people kowtowing to him, especially women.

Closing his eyes, he tried to put a face to the coolly
competent voice and came up with one which looked
suspiciously like his mother when she'd been younger,
his black-haired, black-eyed beautiful mother, his sleekly
sophisticated and treacherously adulterous mother!

Jordan scowled, then snapped forward on his chair,
determined to get his mind back on work, and off Mrs
Merrick of Coastal Properties. But it was no use. His
curiosity over the woman was far too aroused.

Or was it something else?

He frowned, then swore. Yes, dammit. That was it.
That was definitely it. Somehow, Mrs Merrick's voice—
or was it her challenging attitude?—had sparked a sexual
response in him. God knew how. It was crazy, really.
Quite crazy.

But, crazy or not, he couldn't sit in his damned office
another moment. He had to see for himself the face
behind the voice, had to see if reality would live up to
fantasy.

And if it did?

His conscience stabbed at him as he put on his jacket
and felt for his car keys in the pocket. The woman was
married. He himself was on the verge of becoming engaged, to a very beautiful young lady who gave him
everything he'd ever wanted from a woman. Total attention. Adoration. Sex—when he had time for it. She
never complained or demanded. She was sweet and accommodating. She was perfection.

She wouldn't change if he married her, either. He was
confident of that. Erica was one of those females who

considered being a wife a career in itself. Exactly his cup of tea.

So what the hell are you doing, jumping up and running off to see some woman, just because she has a sexy voice? You don't mean to do anything about it, do you? *Do* you?

Suddenly, he wasn't at all sure of that, either.

His grimace reflected this highly uncharacteristic inner torment. It wasn't like him to be unsure of anything. He'd always known exactly what he wanted in life, and was on the verge of having it all.

Now here he was, being besieged by the most ridiculous—and potentially dangerous—impulse. Common sense warned him to buy a weekender from another real-estate agent in Blackrock Beach; there were several listed in the phone book. But somehow common sense had no power against his intense desire to see the woman he'd just hung up on in the flesh. No power at all.

He mocked himself with a dry laugh as he hurried towards the lift. With a bit of luck, Mrs Merrick wouldn't be anything at all like the coolly beautiful creature she sounded. Voices could be very deceiving. She would probably turn out to be a hard-faced middle-aged hag with about as much sex appeal as Ma Kettle.

Jordan hoped so. He really did.

A glance at his watch showed ten past ten. He'd told her he'd be there by lunchtime. If he put his foot down, he might make it before twelve...

Bonnie heaved a weary sigh, shaking her head as her eyes wandered back to the phone, now lying silent on her desk.

I didn't handle that at all well, she thought regretfully. I let the man niggle me from the first moment, when he

assumed I wasn't one of the sales staff, merely because
I was a woman.

Training had stopped her short of being rude, but there
was no denying the coolness in her voice, or the pique
behind her offer to transfer him over to one of the men.

Fortunately, he hadn't called her bluff. She could do
with an easy sale to start the week, after spending the
whole weekend in bed with a tummy bug. Bonnie had
topped the sales figures for the previous month, and had
been hoping to repeat the performance for November.

Which meant she could hardly afford to look gift-
horses in the mouth, and Mr Moneybags had sounded
like a gift-horse.

What was his name, now? Vine-Hall. Yes, that was
it. Vine-Hall. The name suited him. Pompous and
arrogant!

'That's quite a scowl, love. Are you sure you should
have come back to work this morning?'

Bonnie smiled up at the tall, lean man standing beside
her desk. Gary was the only one of her male colleagues
not at all undermined by her recent sales success. Forty-
five and happily married, he was a genuinely nice man
with a very relaxed personality and no ambition to do
anything but make enough money to live on. Which he
did nicely.

'I couldn't bear another minute in that house by
myself,' she answered truthfully. She hadn't realised till
yesterday how much she hated the place, forty-eight
hours without a break within its walls bringing back that
claustrophobic feeling of imprisonment which had
swamped her during the last year of her three-year
marriage.

Gary was frowning down at her. 'You're awfully pale,'
he said. 'And you have dark rings under your eyes. Come
on, I think you could do with a fortifying cup of coffee.'

'I'll go for that,' she said, and stood up to accompany Gary down to the back room and the coffee-machine.

'You've lost weight as well,' he said as he went about making coffee for both of them.

'Now I really like the sound of that.'

'You're not fat, Bonnie,' he chided.

Maybe not, she thought, but having a womanly shape did have its drawbacks. Bonnie had found that in the male-dominated business world of real estate voluptuous curves could be more of a burden than an asset. When buying clothes nowadays, her first consideration was always whether the outfit would minimise her figure, not emphasise it.

The linen suit she was wearing that morning was a typical choice. A bland cream colour, it had a straight but not too tight skirt and a long, gently shaped jacket which could be kept buttoned up without restriction, the deep V-neckline filled modestly with a gold silk camisole the same colour as her hair.

'I could do with less in certain areas,' she said ruefully as she took the steaming mug Gary offered her.

'Not from a man's point of view.'

A reproachful glance from Bonnie only brought a nonchalant shrug. 'I might be married, but I can still look.'

'Just so long as that's all you do.'

'I'm not Neil, love.'

Bonnie sighed and sipped her coffee.

'Is he still bothering you?' Gary asked.

'Not for the moment.' He'd temporarily stopped asking her out, but only after she'd turned him down a zillion times. But Neil was the persistent type. He was also under the illusion that a widow was always a good mark, especially a young, attractive one who, to all in-

tents and purposes, had not had a man in her bed for
three years.

'I'd watch him if I were you,' Gary murmured.

'What do you mean by that?'

'I've come across blokes like Neil before. They don't
like losing...at anything.'

Bonnie nodded wryly. 'So I've gathered.'

'He was most put out at the meeting this morning when
the boss spent more time fussing over your health than
praising him for his weekend sales.'

'Yes, I noticed that.'

'Edgar did too, and he didn't seem too happy with
Neil's attitude. Why do you think he kept him back
afterwards?'

Bonnie grimaced. 'He'll only make things worse if he
says anything.'

'My feelings exactly. That's why I thought I'd give
you a quiet warning. Neil's not likely to take a dressing-
down too well. Thankfully, he's heading the figures this
month so far. It might be better if he stays there,' Gary
finished with a meaningful look.

Bonnie blinked her astonishment. 'Are you suggesting I deliberately let him win?'

'It might be the wisest course of action. Edgar isn't
going to fire Neil, love. He's a top salesman. Life could
get very awkward for you around here, however, if you
keep making our young stud feel a failure in more ways
than one. He's only a baby, you know, and not used to
rejection in the female department.'

'He's twenty-five, same as me,' she grumbled. 'About
time he grew up a bit.' Despite Gary's suggestion
sounding sensible, something very strong within Bonnie
rebelled at the idea of holding back in deference to male
ego. She'd spent her entire marriage doing that, and the

damage to her self-esteem had been enormous. It went against the grain just to let Neil win. It really did!

Gary took her silence for agreement. 'You could waste a nice lot of time trying to sell that dear old house which just came on the listings this morning. You know...the one perched on the bluff between here and Cairncross Bay.'

'That monstrosity! It would take a magic wand to sell that place!'

Gary laughed. 'Exactly. I've actually got the photo in my pocket here, since it's my unenviable job to write a spiel for the window display. How shall I describe it?' he joked as he held it out in front of him. 'A handyman's delight?'

She glanced down at it and shook her head. Lord, it looked like something out of *The Munsters*! Twostoreyed and wooden, the house had odd turret-like projections, large black chimneys, and small pokey windows. Add to that its ramshackle condition and the overgrown garden surrounding it, and images of ghosts weren't far away.

Edgar had told them it was reputedly haunted. Bonnie didn't wonder. And shuddered anew.

'Who on earth is going to buy a dump like that?' she mused aloud as she stared down at it.

'An eccentric recluse with a passion for Frankenstein?' came Gary's mocking suggestion.

'Very funny. We could have easily unloaded it to a developer for the fifteen fantastic acres it's sitting on if it hadn't been for that stupid covenant on the title stipulating that the house and land have to remain intact.'

'True,' Gary agreed drily. 'We might even have gotten the ridiculous three hundred thousand they're asking for it.'

'Edgar said they might accept two hundred and fifty thousand.'

The house was a deceased estate, the current owner having inherited it from his aunt who'd dropped dead of a stroke in a local supermarket only the previous week. A Mrs McClelland. Seventy-five years old and batty as they came, according to the nephew and heir. He'd informed Edgar it was just as well she didn't die in the house because no one would have found her for months. Apparently she was something of a hermit. Refused to leave the place because she said the spirits of her dead husband and baby lived there. The nephew wanted the place sold as quickly as possible. He'd cleared away all the personal effects, cutlery, crockery and such, but was willing to sell the rest as was, with the furniture inclusive.

If the furniture was anything like the house, Bonnie thought ruefully, it would hardly be a selling factor.

'No one could sell this place for that price,' she pronounced firmly.

'Just the thing, then,' Gary said drily, 'to waste your time and ensure your figures don't pass Neil's. Daphne has the keys at Reception. Why don't you fill in the morning having a look at it?'

'Oh, I don't know, Gary. I'm not sure I could stomach just letting Neil win.'

'Suit yourself. But don't say you haven't been warned.'

Gary had just wandered off back to his desk when the object of their discussion strode into the backroom.

There was no doubt Neil was handsome, Bonnie conceded. But brother, did he know it. A real peacock, he was always preening himself by combing his thick blond hair or straightening the loud ties he favoured. On spotting her standing by the coffee-machine, his blue eyes narrowed. He stared, first at her body, and then at her hair.

Bonnie groaned silently, regretting her decision to leave her hair half down that day. Over the years, her hair had caused her as much, perhaps even more trouble than her figure. A flamboyant gold colour, its naturally tight curls made it impossible to style. She hated it short yet, long, it grew in a wild spiralled abundance which, when left totally out, gave her an untamed look that men were quick to misinterpret.

'I suppose I should have guessed,' came Neil's cryptic mutter as he stalked over to snatch a mug down out of the automatic dispenser.

'Guessed what?'

'That you're having it off with the boss.'

Bonnie was speechless. OK, so Edgar Gray was a womaniser. Everyone in Blackrock Beach knew that. Even at fifty, with his receding hairline and spreading waistline, he still had considerable success with the opposite sex. Women liked him and he had three ex-wives to prove it. Even Bonnie liked him, but only as her boss. Edgar had always had the good sense not to cross the invisible line she had drawn up the day he'd hired her.

'You might think you can pull the wool over everyone else's eyes around here with your cool touch-me-not act,' Neil swept on nastily, 'but I used to drink at the same pub as your hubby on a Friday night, and I know just what you are. He used to worry himself sick that you were seeing men behind his back. *Men*, honey. Not a man. You're a closet nympho, Bonnie Merrick. I know it and you know it. I just didn't think you'd sleep with an old geyser like Edgar. I thought a hot-looking bird like yourself would be more selective.'

All the blood had drained from Bonnie's face. She tried to say something, tried to deny Neil's appalling accusations, but she could not seem to find her voice.

Neil laughed at her shocked expression. 'You've got it down pat, haven't you? That wide-eyed innocent look. I'll bet you fooled your husband real good to begin with, just like you fooled me here for a while. You know, I always wondered why Edgar hired you, a girl with no sales experience at all. But you had the experience he was looking for, didn't you?'

'You're mad!' she blurted out. 'Do you realise if I told Edgar what you've just said he'd fire you?'

'You think so, honey? I doubt it. Even if by some remote possibility I was wrong, dear old Edgar would be so flattered. After I apologised sincerely then told him it was all an honest enough mistake, he'd give me another lecture while underneath he'd be cock-a-hoop that people still thought he was such a stud.'

'You're insane!'

'Heck, no, honey, I've never been saner. I knew there had to be a good reason why you kept turning me down. Now I know why. It's nothing personal. It's just business, isn't it? I reckon I've also finally figured out how come you've become such a whiz at selling houses. When a guy buys a place from you, he gets a bonus, doesn't he? One thing I'd like to know, though: do you screw the sucker before he signs on the dotted line or after?'

Bonnie almost threw her coffee all over him. At the last second, she gave him a contemptuous glare then whirled away to pour it down the sink. Without looking back, she marched back to her desk where she snatched up her bag and car keys before sweeping on to Reception.

'Daphne, has Edgar given you the keys to the McClelland place yet?' she asked the receptionist whose job it was to keep all the keys.

'Yes, I think so. Yes, here they are. The address is written on the tag. I have no idea where that road is, though, do you?'

'Edgar gave us all detailed directions so we wouldn't get lost. Apparently, it's only five minutes from here but tucked away down a deserted bush track.'

'Is that where you're off to now?'

'Sure is.'

It was only ten-thirty. Mr Plum-in-the-mouth Moneybags Vine-Hall wouldn't arrive before twelve at the earliest. She'd make sure she was back by then with her best the-client-is-always-right smile in place, plus a possible decision over what she was going to do about Neil.

Meanwhile, she badly needed a breath of fresh air.

'Going to show it to that man who rang from Sydney a little while ago?' Daphne enquired eagerly.

'Good lord, no. No, I'm not expecting *him* till lunchtime. I should definitely be back by then but if, for some weird and wonderful reason, I'm delayed, look after him for me, will you? His name's Vine-Hall.'

'My pleasure,' Daphne cooed. 'His voice was yummy.'

Bonnie laughed at her youthful optimism. Daphne was only nineteen. 'My experience with yummy male telephone voices,' she informed the bubbly brunette, 'is that they're connected to very fat, very bald and very un-yummy men. Mr Vine-Hall, I can assure you, will prove to be a very disappointing specimen of the male species.'

CHAPTER TWO

BONNIE'S frustration was momentarily forgotten the second she stepped out of the office on to the pavement and glanced across the main street to the beach beyond.

Blackrock Beach on a clear sunny day was something to behold. The sparkling blue sea, the clean white sands, the stately Norfolk pines in the foreground, the rugged cliffs curving round at each end of the beach—it was a view bar none. Bonnie had lived most of her life here and she couldn't imagine living anywhere else.

Sighing, she turned and strode round to the car park behind the office, wishing as she went that Neil Campion lived somewhere else. Today, he'd moved from being a minor irritation in her life to a major problem. Bonnie wasn't sure what to do about him yet, but she knew one thing. She wasn't going to let him win this month's sales competition. No, siree. The pewter mug for November was going to sit on her mantelpiece alongside October's if it was the last thing she did.

Her decision to visit the McClelland house this morning was not just to get away from Neil. Neither was it to waste time. She was determined to find some way—some angle—of selling that monstrosity. They had few enough new listings this month and she couldn't afford to waste a single opportunity.

It was to be thanked for that she hadn't totally alienated Mr Moneybags earlier on. Imagine having stupidly handed him over to someone else. Daphne would probably have put him through to Neil. Bonnie shuddered at the thought.

Five minutes later, she was turning her Ford Falcon on to the narrow dirt track which led down to the McClelland house, grimacing when a cloud of dust rose from under the wheels to settle over the shiny green paintwork. Darn. Now she would have to take Mr Vine-Hall around in a dirty car. How irritating!

Bonnie automatically eased her foot off the accelerator, which was just as well because the surface was like corrugated iron. The thought of bringing clients down this excuse for a road was daunting enough, but when it came to an abrupt end in front of the oldest, tallest and rustiest pair of iron gates Bonnie had ever seen she just stared in disbelief.

Edgar hadn't mentioned the gates. Or the crumbling stone wall. Neither were they in the photograph. Bonnie could well understand why. The house beyond was bad enough but, combined with the Count Dracula gates, the whole caboodle would give anyone the willies.

Shaking her head, she climbed out of the car and peered through the rusty rungs at the house itself. Under a bright November sun it didn't look nearly as spooky as it had in the photograph, but still, it was hardly inviting. The once white walls were a grimy grey, with paint peeling off them. Something green and fungusy was growing all over the roof. The guttering was drooping in places and the garden, if one could call it a garden, was an overgrown disaster area.

A small laugh bubbled up in her throat as she imagined what Mr Vine-Hall would say if she showed him this place as a possible weekender. Still, it did have his two stated requirements. It was sure to have an ocean view from the upstairs windows, and Edgar had said there was a cliff trail somewhere which led down to a small private cove.

Since money was no object, then Mr Moneybags could pour plenty into having the place done up and the grounds restored. Actually, if one had some imagination, it might not look half bad. The house itself had a quirky sense of character which was missing from modern homes. As for the grounds…well, at least there was plenty of them!

Of course, not everyone wanted to live with a couple of ghosts, Bonnie conceded ruefully to herself. Maybe there were three of them, now that the lady of the house had passed away as well.

When the gates creaked alarmingly as she pushed them open, Bonnie decided it was as well she didn't believe in ghosts. Otherwise coming here alone might have unnerved her.

Actually, she didn't feel totally calm as she drove the car through the gateway and up to the house. All those small dark windows. Maybe someone was watching her through one of them.

Shrugging off her fanciful thoughts as ridiculous, she climbed out of the car and walked up the three cracked stone steps on to the wide but rickety front veranda. One of the planks creaked ominously underfoot, sending a shiver running down her spine.

Now stop this, she told herself firmly, and, squaring her shoulders, stepped up to the front door. Bonnie resisted the impulse to clang the iron knocker up and down to frighten away anyone or anything that might be inside. Instead, she inserted the large brass key and prepared herself for a fight to get the old lock open.

When the key turned with surprising ease, she was reminded that till recently this house had been lived in. Just because it looked as if it had been standing there forlorn and unused for years and years, it didn't mean it was so. Bonnie swung open the door, determined not to allow herself to be besieged by any further fanciful thoughts.

Her first impression was one of darkness and mustiness, but once she'd snapped on the light the hallway was bathed in a soft warm glow, making the worn strip of patterned carpet quite welcoming. The sense of cosiness increased as she ventured further inside, and it was with an air of expectation—but no eeriness—that Bonnie continued on through the house.

The first door leading off the hallway to the left revealed a formal sitting-room, or parlour, as it was once called. None of the furniture qualified as valuable antiques, Bonnie observed, but it was all rather quaint. She wandered through the room, running a gentle hand over the backs of the chintz-covered armchairs and ignoring the cobwebs in the corners.

A pair of louvred doors led into what could only be described as a morning-room or sun-room. It was surprisingly light, with a large window and pale polished floors. An old roll-top desk stood against one wall, a battered oak sideboard against another. The sun was streaming on to a round wooden table under the window and it occurred to Bonnie that to breakfast in such a room would be a marvellous start to the day.

She moved on, opening the only exit door to find herself in a long rectangular kitchen which was a real horror. An ancient electric stove was the only reasonably modern appliance in sight. There wasn't even a refrigerator. Lord knew how that poor old woman had managed without one.

The kitchen led into a dining-room on the other side of the house, which, in turn, was connected through another pair of louvred doors to a library-cum-study. This was a most attractive room, despite its carpet being threadbare, the velvet curtains mouldy, the leather chairs worn, and the bookshelves more full of dust than books.

The whole place had potential, she decided as she climbed the rather narrow staircase. And charm. She liked it. Surely someone else would like it too?

Upstairs, the main bedroom ran the entire length of the left side of the house. But it was empty except for a large brass bed covered in a hand-crocheted cream quilt. Clearly old Mrs McClelland hadn't used the main bedroom, despite its not smelling musty in there at all. It did, in fact, carry a faint whiff of lavender. She went over and sniffed at the pillows. Yes ... lavender.

The bathroom that came off the landing at the top of the stairs was as antiquated as the kitchen. Bonnie shook her head at the chipped enamel bath on legs, and the tiny washbasin with its plug on a chain. The separate toilet had a chain for flushing as well. This brought a smile till she remembered these were the very things that would make the house difficult to sell.

Only two rooms were left upstairs, both coming off a narrow L-shaped gallery on the right side of the stairwell.

For some unaccountable reason Bonnie walked past the nearest to open the other.

It was clearly the room the old lady had slept in, despite the lack of personal effects. The furniture was dark and heavy, the rug alongside the single bed worthy of being on the endangered species list, the patchwork quilt having seen better days. The whole room was depressing, she thought, and quickly shut the door.

Which left only one room to inspect. Bonnie walked swiftly back along the narrow hallway, wanting suddenly to be done with the house, yet when her hand reached to turn this last remaining knob she hesitated. An odd nervousness claimed her and she almost turned and walked away. Then something—some force much stronger than fear—impelled her wrist to turn.

After she let the knob go, the door seemed to open by itself, creaking slowly wide. With her heart in her mouth, Bonnie took a tremulous step inside, scooping in a startled breath as her eyes travelled around the room. The tentacles of some indefinable emotion wrapped themselves around her heart and squeezed tight, bringing with it an incredible wave of sadness.

It was a nursery.

Heavy legs carried her further into the room, shaking fingers creeping out to touch the white cradle, swinging it back and forth, back and forth. Her stomach twisted as she gazed at the purity of the snow-white sheets, the delicacy of the pink and white motifs sewn on to the pillow-case. She wanted to cry when she picked up the handmade toys, crafted with such love and attention to detail. And when she opened the baby-record book on top of the chest of drawers, the sudden constriction in her chest only reinforced what she already knew.

It was empty.

Not a word had been entered in that sad, sad testament. One glance had told Bonnie that this nursery had never been occupied. There were no chips on the white furniture, no marks on the wallpaper, no tell-tale damage to the toys.

Sympathy swelled her heart as she thought of old Mrs McClelland. What unfulfilled dreams lay in this room? What heartache?

Her eyes brimmed with sudden tears. Hastily she blinked them away and moved towards the large bay window that gave a perfect view of the ocean. The sun was quite hot through the glass and she flicked open the buttons of her jacket as she stood there, drinking in the view and willing herself to think happier thoughts.

But nothing could distract her from an overwhelming feeling of grief. Finally, her eyes dropped away, and she found herself peering down at the old-fashioned window-seat and the definite hollow in the padded seat.

Realisation jerked her back upright. Good God, she thought shakily. This was where the old lady used to sit and the impression of her body still lingered. How many hours had that poor woman spent here? How many times had she been drawn to this spot?

Something strangely compelling pulled Bonnie down till she was also sitting there, her back against the wooden window-frame, her green eyes glazing as they travelled along the same path those weary old eyes had travelled... into the past.

Only this time the past was Bonnie's...

Keith had been getting ready for work that final day, buttoning up his policeman's uniform, looking as handsome and dashing as ever. She'd watched him from where she lay, huddled up under the sheets, still not able to believe what had happened the night before.

It wasn't that Keith had never hit her before. He had. But only with his hand, and never more than once, or twice.

But last night...

Oh, God, she could hardly bear to remember. The pain had been excruciating. It was *still* excruciating.

When he came over and sat down on the side of the bed, she couldn't help cringing away from him.

'Don't be like that, Bonnie,' he reproached. 'It wasn't my fault, you know. You made me lose my temper. Why didn't you just tell me where you went yesterday in the first place? I knew you weren't shopping. There were too many miles on the speedometer. You should have admitted you'd driven up to Morriset to visit your sister in the first place. I don't mind you visiting Louise, as long as you ask permission first. If you'd done that, there would have been no reason for you to lie, and no reason for me to punish you for it.'

Bonnie stared at him, her head dizzy with fear.

'Promise me you'll ask permission next time,' he said, cupping her chin and squeezing tight.

Her heart began to thud.

'I want to hear you say it, Bonnie,' he snarled. 'Say, I promise I will ask permission next time.'

'I...I promise I'll ask permission next time,' she choked out, her throat dry, her tongue thick.

'Good girl.'

When he lowered his mouth to give her an obscenely deep kiss, his hands slipping under the sheets to play with her breasts at the same time, she was almost sick. When his mouth lifted and he began pinching one of her nipples, watching coldly while the pain registered in her eyes, she wanted to kill him.

'Just a little reminder of what you can expect if you lie to me again,' he warned before standing up abruptly and striding from the room. 'Make sure you're here when I get home,' he called back over his shoulder.

She would never know if she would have been home at the end of that day, because Keith never came home. He was killed that morning, during a car chase, at an intersection. One of his colleagues called at the house soon afterwards to give her the bad news. He thought her tears were tears of grief, but he was wrong. They were tears of relief.

CHAPTER THREE

JORDAN studied the rough map that the chap at Coastal Properties had given him before gunning the engine of his car and driving off in search of the increasingly enigmatic Mrs Merrick.

His disappointment when he'd found out she wasn't in the office had been sharp. But his unexpectedly early arrival had drawn some interesting information which he might not otherwise have gleaned about the woman.

Her dashing young colleague had not hidden his contempt for her business ethics, suggesting with a smirk that Jordan was a very lucky man to have someone like Mrs Merrick 'handle' him. Wink wink, nudge nudge, say no more.

The various implications would have been clear to a brain-dead moron. A queen's counsel certainly did not need to have it beaten into his head with a hammer.

Mrs Merrick, in her workmate's opinion, was obviously not above using her physical assets when trying to make a sale. Jordan wasn't sure if he was repelled or excited by that thought. It would seem likely that the lady must have some special assets worth trading on if she did business that way. In his experience, females with lax morals were pretty well always easy on the eye.

Yet tramps had never held any fascination for him. And he'd come across a good few in his thirty-six years.

If she *was* a tramp, that was. He'd found that people eager to offer unsought-after information about others were often lying. Or at least exaggerating. He resolved

24

to keep an open mind on the subject of Mrs Merrick's morals.

It took him a good ten minutes to find the dirt road, having driven right past it the first time. His patience was wearing thin by the time he made it down the rough track and up to what must have been the weirdest, ugliest old house he had ever seen. Parking next to a green Falcon, he climbed out, did up his suit jacket and dragged in a deep breath.

The moment of truth had come...

Bonnie sighed softly as she sat on in that room of dreams, mindless of time passing. It was as if she had entered another world where time stood still, where people could rest a while before picking up the strands of their lives again.

What first roused her from her trance-like state? Was it a sound, or the draught that suddenly chilled her legs? She stiffened in the window-seat, her eyelids fluttering nervously as they became fixed on the open doorway. Her ears strained to catch any more sounds but instantly all was very, very quiet.

Then she heard them. Unmistakable footsteps on the stairs, coming closer...closer...each soft thud a warning for her to move, to get up, to investigate. Her eyes grew wider as the footsteps reached the top of the stairs, turned, then moved inexorably towards the nursery. Her heart began hammering wildly against her chest.

When a tall, dark figure loomed into the dimly lit rectangle that was the doorway, even her breathing ceased. All she could do was stare, her eyes round, her lips parted. Common sense told her this was not some ghost, come to haunt her. But her mind was too far from reality to grasp that fact sufficiently, to act upon it. And so she sat frozen on that window-seat, struggling to get some breath back into her stunned body.

Jordan could do nothing but stare, every muscle within his body having gone rigid with shock.

Dear God...

He'd expected a beauty of some sort, especially after his encounter with that chap from the office. But his mental picture of Mrs Merrick had shifted from a classy, sleek-haired brunette to a cheap, brassy blond. He certainly hadn't been expecting an angel.

Yet that was exactly what she looked like sitting there in the sunlight... a gloriously golden angel. His breath caught in his throat as she lifted her chin slightly, and the rays of the sun caused a halo effect behind her head.

He took a startled step forward, a shift in the light allowing him to focus on the details of her face. Once again, he had to smother a gasp of shock. For there was nothing angelic about that face.

Oh, it was lovely all right. Exquisitely so. But there was something about those widely spaced green eyes and sinfully lush mouth which made one think of hell, not heaven, sin, not virtue, temptation, not restraint.

Suddenly, he wanted to pull her to her feet, drag her into his arms and bury his face into everything she was...and promised to be...from her hair to her breasts to her...

When the stranger took an abrupt step forward and his facial features broke into the light, Bonnie drew in a sharp breath.

Dear heaven, she thought shakily. She had come across a couple of exceptionally good-looking men in her life— her husband had been one of them—but this was something else. This man gave tall, dark and handsome new meaning.

But it wasn't just his looks that held her momentarily captive. There was an intensity about him, especially in those deeply set dark eyes which were at that moment locked on her own. She could not stop staring at him. Neither could she find her voice. The seconds ticked away and the room started to swim around her. She tried to break her eyes away, but could not seem to find the strength, or will-power.

'Mrs Merrick from Coastal Properties, I presume,' the object of her staring said at last in a strangely cold voice.

It was enough to snap Bonnie out of herself, though not with as much instant composure as she would have liked.

'Yes...yes...that's right...that's me,' she said, slipping from the window-seat on to slightly numb feet. When a long golden curl came loose to fall across her right eye, she quickly looped it back behind her ear and drew in a deep, steadying breath.

'And who might you be?' she returned, hoping she sounded a darn sight calmer than she felt. Her rattled brain struggled to find the identity of this man who not only knew her name and place of employment, but who felt he had the right to walk into this house uninvited and unannounced.

Inspiration struck in a rush. 'Oh, of course!' she exclaimed 'You must be Mrs McClelland's nephew.'

The handsome stranger made no attempt to confirm this guess, or to come further forward. He slid his hands into the trouser pockets of his navy pin-striped suit and proceeded to survey her with unnerving attention to detail, his eyes sweeping slowly down her body, lingering on where her cream jacket was lying open at the front.

Bonnie's chest tightened with dismay. It took all of her self-control not to grab the lapels of her jacket and hold the garment defensively closed across her chest.

For she wasn't wearing a bra.

Frankly, she never wore one if she was wearing a suit with a lined jacket, simply because she looked less busty without one. Since she normally never undid her jacket at work, no one ever noticed. All she had to remember to do was not walk too fast. And what woman did that in high heels?

When the man's gaze remained cool, not lascivious in any way, Bonnie felt some relief. But not enough for her to relax totally.

'No, I am not Mrs McClelland's nephew,' the stranger informed her in an upper-crust accent. 'I'm Jordan Vine-Hall. Your office directed me here. I did call out to you downstairs but you didn't answer.'

Bonnie's heart sank. Oh, God. Mr Moneybags himself! And she hadn't been at the office to meet him.

Any dismay was quickly overridden by a surge of the same irritation he'd engendered in her during their earlier phone call. What right had he to drive up here so darned quickly? And why couldn't he have been fat and bald? Why did he have to be the most impressive-looking man in the Southern hemisphere, maybe even the whole world? Lord, Daphne would have a field day when she got back to the office!

'You shouldn't have come out all this way, Mr Vine-Hall,' she said extra-coolly in an attempt to hide her inner fluster. 'I would have been back at the office by twelve.'

'It's just on twelve now, Mrs Merrick.'

A quick glance at her wristwatch brought a gasp of shock. 'Good heavens, so it is! I... I lost track of time. I'm so sorry, Mr Vine-Hall. I don't know what to say.'

Bonnie hated having to grovel, but she could see that a little grovelling was called for.

'No need to apologise,' he drawled. 'As I said, I was early.'

'I hope you didn't have too much trouble finding me.'

'I had good directions. Your—er—friend was most helpful.'

'Oh, what friend was that?'

'I think his name was Neil.'

The memory of the morning's encounter with Neil swept back in and Bonnie grimaced. Whatever was she going to do about him? Should she tell Edgar or try to brazen the situation out?

'Something wrong, Mrs Merrick?'

Bonnie was jerked back to the present. 'No, no, I was just wondering where to take you first. I suppose you wouldn't be interested in this place, would you?'

His face told it all.

'I didn't think so,' she muttered drily. 'Would you—um—mind waiting outside while I lock up?'

He glared at her for a second, then spun round and stalked off, leaving Bonnie with the impression of extreme irritation.

Her sigh carried a weary acceptance that the week might not start with an easy sale after all. Still, she supposed he had some right to be annoyed, coming all this way from Sydney then having to traipse out here after her, when he'd probably expected her to be there at the office, ready and waiting to dance attention on him. Wealthy men liked a lot of attention, she'd found.

Bonnie touched a slightly shaking hand to her head and glanced around the nursery. It was this room's fault, she decided. She hadn't wanted to come in here. She should have listened to her intuition. She should certainly have never sat down in that window-seat.

Somehow, by doing so, the old woman's pain had become her pain, filling Bonnie's soul with a nameless yearning. It filled her now, yet remained tantalisingly out of reach.

What *was* it the old woman wanted her to do?

Bonnie shook her head. She was being fanciful again, the so-called haunted atmosphere getting to her. She didn't believe in ghosts. She didn't believe in haunted houses, or hidden messages from beyond. Her job here was to find a buyer for this place, not surrender to vague, highly emotional impulses.

Resisting the urge to give the room one last look, Bonnie closed the door and started down the stairs, doing up her jacket as she went. This time, she tried to see the house more as Mr Vine-Hall had and not through sentimental, rose-coloured spectacles.

It was a hideous old place. Run-down. Musty. Poky.

By the time she reached the bottom of the stairs, Bonnie felt oddly depressed.

But depressed salespeople rarely sold houses, so she made a conscious effort to brighten up before stepping outside, plastering a cheery smile on her face.

She needn't have bothered, since her cantankerous client was standing on the veranda with his back to her. Every line in his body spelt impatience and tension, from the rigid set of his shoulders to the wide, feet-apart stance. She suspected he was a man who never relaxed, who lived life at too fast a pace. She wondered, for the second time, what he did for a living, and resolved to find out as soon as she could.

'All set,' she said brightly on joining him at the edge of the veranda.

He turned slowly towards her and once again she was struck by his looks, though up close and on second inspection he was not as conventionally handsome as she had first thought. His face was long and lean, his nose sharp, his mouth stern. It was a rather harsh, ascetic face, softened only by the wave of dark hair across his high forehead, and dominated by a pair of deep-set black eyes which drew one's own eyes to them like a magnet. They had held her, transfixed, up in the nursery. They were holding her now, his gaze piercing, as though he was trying to see right into her very soul.

And what he was seeing was not to his liking.

Or was he always like this? she puzzled. Austere, grim, and coldly disapproving?

'Shall we be using both cars?' he asked curtly.

She noted the sleek bronze sedan parked on the other side of her Falcon. 'I think we should go in mine,' she said sensibly. 'Otherwise we'll waste valuable time.'

'And *my* car?' he asked, his left eyebrow arching sardonically skywards.

'It will be quite safe here,' she assured him, smothering any annoyance. The man definitely had an attitude problem. But she'd dealt with difficult clients before and prided herself on usually being able to bring them round. 'I'll lock the gates on the way out,' she told him, and drummed up a placating smile.

No luck. All it produced was a half-sneer, as though her smile had been a long-awaited mistake.

'But will *I* be safe, Mrs Merrick?' he muttered.

'Pardon?'

Her bewilderment at this cryptic comment seemed to surprise him.

'I usually prefer to drive,' he stated brusquely. 'Do you drive competently, Mrs Merrick?'

'I am a very competent driver,' she snapped, giving in finally to irritation.

'Yes, I'm sure you are,' he said with an odd hint of scorn still in his voice. 'I'm sure you're very competent

at everything you do. Shall we go?' And he strode off
down the steps in the direction of the cars, leaving a
totally thrown Bonnie behind.

She glared after him, wondering what on earth she
had done to get so far on his wrong side. Surely, if he'd
been really annoyed by her not being at the office when
he arrived, he could have demanded that someone else
show him around?

Bonnie found it very frustrating to be on the end of
such disfavour, particularly when she didn't think it jus-
tified. All she could imagine was that Mr Vine-Hall was
even more of a chauvinist than he'd displayed during
his phone call this morning. There was no doubting his
displeasure at having to deal with a woman. *Any* woman.
Perhaps he considered doing business with such a young
one the living end!

That had to be it, she supposed, though a niggling
little something kept telling her there was more to this
situation than met the eye. But what?

Shaking her head, she trailed after the man, thinking
to herself that this was the worst Monday she had encountered in a long, long time. What else could go
wrong?

Mr Vine-Hall was stretched out in the passenger seat
by the time she slid behind the wheel, her automatic
sidewards glance meeting a wary, sour-puss expression.
Those unnerving black eyes flicked over her once more,
and what he saw still didn't seem to meet with his
approval.

'So where are we off to first, Mrs Merrick?' he asked,
that dry note still in his voice.

Bonnie suppressed a sigh and decided to give good
manners and pleasantries one last try. 'Perhaps you'd
better call me Bonnie,' she began with dogged optimism. 'Not many people call me Mrs Merrick.'

'No,' he said slowly. 'I don't imagine they do.'

Once again, Bonnie was taken aback. What on earth was going on here?

But then suddenly he smiled, and she was quite blown away. Not only by the change in his face—from churlish to charming in one second flat—but by the involuntary leap in her heart.

'In that case you must call me Jordan,' he returned smoothly. 'Yes, I think first names are definitely called for, since I have a feeling we're going to be spending quite some time together. I'm a very difficult man to please, you see, Bonnie. You're going to have to earn every cent of your commission with me.'

'I...I'll do my best,' she said, having to battle hard not to show how rattled she was feeling. Mr Vine-Hall's about-face had been astonishing enough, but that was nothing to her own response to it.

She hoped against hope that it was just shock, and not a sexual thing. After Keith, Bonnie had feared good-looking men for a long time, but her experience with Neil—and a couple of others—had begun to reassure her that she was not blindly susceptible to a handsome face.

Now she wasn't so sure. Maybe they'd just been the wrong type of handsome face.

Her panic was instantaneous, fear making her stomach tighten and her heart thud. She found herself staring at that smiling mouth and wondering if its kiss would send her swirling into a sensuous mist, if the stroke of his tongue would ignite her blood, enslaving her senses, making her want whatever he wanted, making her weak as water in his arms.

Heat began to gather in her face, a heat that was as telling as it was embarrassing.

Wrenching her eyes away, she leant forward to fumble the key into the ignition. Totally flustered now, her reversing was disgracefully ragged, her forward acceleration down the driveway not much better, the car shuddering to a rough halt on the other side of the open gates. Bonnie's hand shook as it reached for the doorhandle.

'I'll lock the gates,' her passenger offered abruptly.

Mortified, she sat stiffly behind the wheel while he moved to accomplish what she probably would have fouled up as well. 'Competent', she had claimed to be. A groan escaped her lips at the incompetence she had just displayed.

She watched in the rear-view mirror as he easily pulled the heavy gates shut and snapped the padlock in place. His actions were smooth and uncluttered, performed lithely with the agility of a young athlete. And yet, Bonnie judged, he must be at least thirty-five.

As he turned back to walk towards the car, she tore her gaze away, not wanting to be caught in the act of looking at him again. She could just imagine what he was already thinking.

Self-disgust had her getting a grip on her rampant emotions with a steely resolve. There would be no calling him by his first name. He would remain Mr Vine-Hall no matter how many hours they had to spend together. On top of that, if she found out that her reaction to his smile a moment ago *was* sexual, she would turn him over to Gary faster than one could say Jack Robinson.

Because there was one thing Bonnie *was* sure of. She wasn't ready yet to become involved with another man. The wounds of her relationship with Keith were too recent, too raw. And while logic told her all men were not like Keith, she couldn't envisage trusting any man again with her body, or her life, for a long, long time.

Which meant keeping any unwanted hormonal activity firmly under control!

'Thank you,' she said crisply once the instigator of her internal lecture was resettled, keeping her eyes staunchly on the road ahead. 'One thing I forgot to ask you, Mr Vine-Hall,' she continued as she eased the car into gear and moved slowly down the bumpy road. 'Does this weekender have to be in Blackrock Beach? We do have several very nice properties listed at some of the other local beaches.'

'I *was* thinking of only Blackrock Beach when I rang,' he replied thoughtfully, 'but I can see it's changed a lot. I was picturing the sleepy little seaside spot I used to holiday in as a boy, but it's hardly that any more.'

'No, it's boomed since the expressway was put in from Sydney up to the Central Coast. Hardly a block in view of the beach which hasn't been built on.'

'Yes, so I noticed. So no. . . I won't hold you exclusively to Blackrock Beach. Show me whatever you think might suit. I do like my peace and quiet at the weekend. And a reasonable amount of privacy.'

Bonnie had reached the end of the dirt road by now, and was feeling decidedly better with this businesslike conversation. If she didn't have to look into his undeniably handsome face too much, and he didn't smile at her too often, she should be able to get through this afternoon without any more awkward moments.

'Oh, and Bonnie. . .' His pregnant pause forced her to look over at him.

'Yes?'

'You agreed to call me Jordan, remember?'

And he smiled at her again.

CHAPTER FOUR

GODDAMN it, she was blushing again!

A guilty confusion wiped the smile off Jordan's face. If there was one thing he knew about women of easy virtue it was that they didn't blush when you started coming on to them. Neither did they keep breaking eye contact or become totally flustered.

The truth of the matter quickly sank in. That bastard back at the real-estate office had lied about her. She wasn't a tramp at all. She was a respectable married woman who was too damned sexy-looking for her own good.

It certainly put a different interpretation on her reactions to him. Any hope that she'd been giving him the eye was obliterated. Clearly, her staring was because he must have seemed horribly rude. Hell, he *had* been horribly rude, right from the start!

She wasn't to know he'd been fighting urges which till today had been totally alien to his personality. Good lord, he hadn't surrendered to any form of uncontrollable passion since he was an adolescent! On top of that, the last female on earth he would consider trying to seduce would be a married woman, albeit a supposedly amoral one. He'd seen the pain adultery caused.

Yet that was exactly what he wanted to do. Seduce her.

He'd staunchly resisted temptation at first, only to give in finally, deliberately misinterpreting her offer that he call her by her first name, thinking he only had to turn

on a bit of charm to make her realise he was willing to
go along with whatever was on offer.

Shame was hard on the heels of guilt. Jordan knew
he was no saint—what man was?—but his behaviour
today had been appalling. So the woman was exquisite,
with a voice like cool silk and a body men might kill for.
So what? That was no excuse.

Damn it all, he'd defended men in court who had done
just that, committed crimes of passion over a beautiful
woman. He'd always thought what fools they were. There
were plenty of other beautiful women in the world. Why
ruin their lives over just one? Why not simply walk away
and climb into another bed? What made them so vulnerable to that one particular woman that they could
think of nothing and no one else?

Such obsessions were the result of a sick mind, he used
to believe. Or a weak character. Suddenly, he was gaining
a different perspective on sexual obsession. And he didn't
like it one bit.

Jordan wanted no part of such a weakness, no part
at all!

His inner torment was getting out of hand when his
usual ruthless logic came to his rescue. This obsession—
for want of a better word—was due to nothing more
than an acute case of male frustration. He'd been
working incredibly long hours over the past few weeks.
Why, he hadn't even had a spare hour to write, let alone
make love.

Erica, of course, had been very understanding, which
was only to be expected. Her lack of any real physical
passion was something Jordan actually found re-
assuring. Hell, the last sort of woman he wanted for a
wife would be one who actually *needed* sex. How would
he be able to trust her when this sort of thing happened
after they were married?

He could still remember that awful Saturday afternoon when he'd come home injured from soccer practice, only to stumble across his mother 'entertaining' a man who wasn't his father on the sofa. He'd been just fifteen and up till then had thought his mother little short of a saint.

He'd stood there, white-faced and shaken, while she'd scrambled into some clothes and shuffled the man out of the back door. When she'd returned to face her son, she'd launched into a muddled explanation, all the while floods of tears running down her flushed cheeks.

Jordan had listened to her pleas for understanding with a chilled heart. She'd claimed she still loved his father but that he was hardly ever home, his ambition to become a judge taking up all his spare time. She'd sobbed that she needed company, *needed* to be loved.

Needed to be screwed, more like it, he'd decided, having seen the man she'd chosen for her lover. He'd been very good-looking and very common, with tattoos over his arms. Not the type to know much about love, only sex.

She'd begged him not to tell his father, and he hadn't. But someone else must have, for he'd overheard his parents having a bitter row that night.

Nothing was ever the same after that. His parents hadn't divorced, but an air of cold remoteness had descended on their relationship which never thawed. Adultery had destroyed his parents' marriage, plus his own respect for his mother. It was the ultimate betrayal, in his opinion, and Jordan wanted no part of it!

He decided then and there to ask Erica to marry him this very night. Make the commitment official, after which he would sweep her off to bed. *That* should set his equilibrium to right!

'By all means call me Mr Vine-Hall, if you're more comfortable with that,' Jordan resumed, his tone crisp.

'I wouldn't like you to think I was trying to come on to a married woman.'

Bonnie swallowed. *Had* she been thinking that? Admittedly, she'd been flustered by his suddenly being nice to her, but she hadn't really stopped to find a reason for it. Her brain seemed to have been scrambled by his smile along with her body.

She steeled herself and looked over at him. He was no longer smiling, but when their eyes met an electric charge seemed to sizzle across the space between them, making her stomach tighten and her breasts prickle alarmingly. Intuition told her that he *would* come on to her if she weren't a married woman.

Tell him you're not married, whispered an insidious little voice. Tell him you're a widow.

She clenched her jaw underneath the force of the temptation, shuddering inside as she remembered where her carnal weaknesses had led her last time—to hell and back. No way could she risk such treatment again. No way. Let him continue to think she was married. It was the only wise course of action.

'Of course I don't think that, Jordan,' she said, amazing herself at the cool tone she'd found in her desperation. 'I can recognise a gentleman when I see one. Now, there's a place at Bateau Bay which I'd like to show you. The lady who owns it is sure to be home and doesn't mind if I drop in at any time.'

His returning smile was rather wry, she thought, but infinitely preferable to his earlier, disturbingly sensual offering. 'I'm totally at your disposal,' he said.

Bonnie managed to keep a straight face, despite her decidedly x-rated thoughts. God, she was wicked. Wicked and weak. She'd been afraid this would happen to her one day. No, not afraid—terrified! She'd always known it was still there, deadly and dormant, despite those last months of marriage having seemingly frozen every desire for sex she had ever had.

OK, so it had taken an exceptional man to melt her ice, but still ... that ice had proven to be a disconcertingly thin layer. Try as she might, she couldn't stop her mind skittering from one erotic image to another, couldn't stop her body flooding with a sexual awareness that was both appalling yet insidiously exciting.

Hating herself, she carefully put on her right-hand indicator and headed north.

Jordan didn't like the first place she showed him. Too large, he said. Or the second. Too small. Or the third. Too noisy. The fourth seemed to find some favour, though he would not be drawn into over-effusiveness. By this time it was half-past one and when he suggested that they stop somewhere for a bite to eat Bonnie reluctantly agreed. Already, time spent with the man had increased her awareness of his physical attractions. Added to that was an admiration of the man himself, and what he did for a living.

He was a barrister. Not an ordinary barrister, either. A queen's counsel. It was no wonder he was impressive, not only in his looks but his general bearing. Never had Bonnie seen a man carry himself with such superb aplomb. Or was the word panache?

Whatever, there was no doubt he was the most self-contained, self-possessed man she had ever come across, not to mention the most attractive. The prospect of just the two of them having an intimate little lunch together was daunting indeed. But she could hardly object. Besides, she was starving herself.

They ended up at a café in a small shopping square in Erina which had umbrellaed tables outside in the sun and a delightful little menu. Bonnie chose a vegetable

pie with a side-salad and coffee, Jordan opting for the
same, but with chips and a bread roll included.

'Have you been selling real estate long?' was his first
question after they'd given their orders.

'Two years,' she admitted, reminding herself to be
careful not to accidentally reveal her widow status. Continuing with the ruse was more difficult than she'd
realised. A couple of times already she'd almost unconsciously given the game away.

'You're good,' he said. 'Refreshingly honest and not
pushy. I'll bet you've been very successful.'

'I have been of late. I even won a pewter mug for best
salesperson last month.'

'Ahh...'

His 'ahh' sparked her curiosity. 'What do you mean
by "ahh"?'

'Nothing, really. Do you work at the weekend?'

'Almost always.'

That eyebrow lifted again. It was a habit of his, she
realised, the gesture carrying a range of expressions from
merely curious to cynical to drily amused to downright
sarcastic. She could well imagine him using it to good
effect in court to undermine a witness's testimony, or as
a clever personal aside with the jury. She could see him
now, setting those jet-black eyes of his on some highly
susceptible woman juror, lifting that eyebrow and immediately creating an intimate little bond between them.

'What about *this* weekend?' he asked. 'Will you be
working this weekend?'

'Yes.'

His frown confused her a little. What was it he wanted
to do this weekend? Surely he wasn't going to ask her
out, not when he thought her a married woman?

Such a prospect should have shocked her. Instead, she
found it unnervingly exciting.

'Right,' he said curtly. 'In that case I'd like to bring my fiancée up this Saturday, once we've narrowed the choices down to a couple of places.'

Bonnie felt the breath leave her lungs in a whoosh. A fiancée... He had a fiancée.

Well, of course he has, you stupid idiot! Either that or a wife. What did you expect? Men like Jordan Vine-Hall don't go round unsnapped up unless they're perennial playboys or gay.

Bonnie suspected she looked as dismayed as she felt. Which was crazy. She should be grateful, since it put him firmly beyond her reach. God, get it together, girl, she told herself firmly. 'What time would you like me to be available?' she asked, avoiding his eyes and struggling to keep her voice steady.

When he didn't answer, she glanced up, only to find him staring at her with narrowed eyes.

'Doesn't your husband find it annoying to have you work every weekend?' he asked sharply.

Bonnie decided there was no point in continuing with this fiasco, which was beginning to be a strain. Besides, what would happen if someone back at the office let the cat out of the bag? She would look a fool.

'I'm sorry,' she said simply. 'I didn't realise you didn't know. I'm a widow. My husband died three years ago.'

Jordan felt as if someone had just punched him in the stomach. A widow. She was a *widow*!

Goddammit, he thought savagely. *Goddammit*!

His fists curled into tight balls and he rubbed them up and down on his thighs under the table, an explosive emotion charging through his veins. If he'd known she was a widow, he would never have mentioned Erica, would never have given her any reason to reject him.

For he had to have her. He could see that now. He'd pretended to himself that he could resist temptation when it would have meant committing adultery, but not even the most noble intention had stopped him still wanting her. It had been building in him all afternoon. The desire. The passion. The need.

Maybe he would have been able to resist in the end. Maybe he would have been able to go away meekly and forget her. But she'd opened the Pandora's box now. She was free, free to accept his advances, free to accept his love.

Love?

Good God, was he mad? He didn't love the woman. He didn't love *any* woman. Love was for adolescents and masochists. He wanted her, that was all. It was sex, nothing more.

This last reaffirmation sent his brain catapulting back to his earlier reasoning that it wasn't Bonnie Merrick he was wanting so badly, but any woman. A night or two in Erica's bed and this insane yearning would quickly become a distant memory.

But what if it didn't? What then, Jordan? What then...?

Bonnie was taken aback by his reaction to her announcement. He looked almost angry. Yet why should he be angry? It didn't make sense.

'You're very young to be a widow,' he said at last, 'let alone one of three years.'

'I'm twenty-five,' she said, rather defensively.

'Was your husband much older?'

'A couple of years.'

'Only a couple of years. What did he die of?'

'He was killed on the job... in a car accident. He was a policeman.'

He mouthed another of those non-committal 'ahh's.

'And children?' he went on after a few seconds'
silence. 'Do you have children?'

'No.' Thank God, she thought. For a while she had
begged Keith to let her have a child, thinking it might
solve their problems, but of course it would have been
the worst thing they could have done. She was grateful
now that he had refused to give her a child, no matter
how sick his reasons.

'Do you regret that?'

'Not really. I was too young to be a mother back then.'

'How old were you when you were married?'

'Nineteen.'

'That *is* young,' he agreed.

Their food arrived at that moment, bringing a welcome
break to what Bonnie was beginning to feel was an inquisition. Perhaps it was the lawyer in him, but when
he asked questions Jordan was very intimidating. It reminded Bonnie uncomfortably of Keith's never-ending
third degrees. She decided it was time to turn the tables.

'So tell me some more about your life, Jordan?' she
asked as she cut her vegetable pie into quarters. 'Why
haven't you married before now?'

'I hadn't met the right woman.'

'And is your fiancée much younger than you?'

'Erica's twenty-four. I'm thirty-six.'

Bonnie detected a curtness in his voice. He didn't want
to talk about his fiancée, this Erica. She wondered why.

'I'll bet you work hard,' she remarked.

'*Too* hard.'

'Which is why you need some place where you can
come and relax.'

His laugh startled her. 'I doubt I'll end up doing much
relaxing up here.'

'I . . . I don't understand.'

He settled those incredible eyes on her and a little shiver ran down her spine. 'I write in my spare time, you see,' he explained, obliterating the sudden ridiculous fear that he was somehow referring to *her*, that he meant to spend his weekends in orgies of wanton behaviour with none other than Mrs Bonnie Merrick, the closet nympho of Blackrock Beach. 'When I write, I hole up in my study and tap away on my PC in a compulsive fervour. Relaxation is far from my mind, which is invariably tormented with all sorts of wild characters and wickednesses.'

'Goodness!' she exclaimed, hoping she wasn't betraying any of her *own* wildly wicked thoughts. 'What on earth do you write? Accounts of the murder trials you've been involved in?' When talking of his work he'd explained that his law firm was ninety per cent criminal defence, mostly on capital cases.

Again he laughed. 'If I tell you, will you promise to keep it a secret?'

'Of course.'

'I write thrillers.'

'But how wonderful! I love thrillers. Have you been published?'

He nodded.

'Would I have read any?'

'I doubt it. I've only had three out so far, under the name of Roger Black. They're all about a lawyer named Richard Halliday who solves the most gruesome crimes. Plenty of sex and violence, with undertones of political anarchy. My publisher thinks the public will love them, but, alas, my family and business colleagues would not.'

'Why not?'

He gave her a look that suggested she knew nothing of his world.

'What about your fiancée?' she persisted, perhaps foolishly. But she was curious about the sort of woman Jordan would choose as his wife. 'What does she think?'

'I haven't told her.'

Bonnie was shocked. 'Why ever not?'

'A secret's not a secret if you tell anyone, is it?'

'But you've just told me!'

That eyebrow arched again as he looked at her, and this time she could not even guess at its meaning. 'Yes, I have, haven't I?' he said quietly.

'*Why* have you?'

His shrug seemed nonchalant but she suspected he was feeling anything but that. 'Maybe I was dying to tell someone and who better than a perfect stranger? One, I might add, who promised to keep my little secret.'

'I can't understand why you keep it a secret at all... from *anyone*! You should be proud of it.'

His look was dry. 'I can see you're a very black and white person, Mrs Merrick. Life isn't always that simple, or clear-cut.'

'Maybe,' she replied, oddly hurt by his words, plus the 'Mrs Merrick' tag. 'But sometimes one needs a bit of black and white to cling to for security. Grey can be a very confusing, clouding colour. Mists are grey,' she said, her eyes glazing as her thoughts drifted from the present to the past. Keith's eyes had been grey too. Grey and cold and cruel...

She shuddered her revulsion, then jumped when Jordan reached over to cover her hand with his. When her eyes lifted to his, he was looking at her with concern. 'I've upset you,' he said. 'I didn't mean to.'

'It's all right,' she said stiffly, all the time hotly aware of that hand covering hers, those long, elegant fingers moving ever so slightly so that her nerve-endings tingled, tiny charges shooting up her arms and down into her breasts.

Her sharply indrawn breath registered in his eyes and his hand closed tightly around hers. 'Bonnie, I——'

'No, don't!' she broke in, and snatched her hand away from under his. 'Please don't,' she repeated in a raw, anguished voice.

Wrenching her eyes away, she stared agitatedly out into the car park that flanked the pavement behind Jordan's chair.

His sigh was weary. 'I was only trying to comfort you.'

'Yes, I know,' she said, keeping her face turned away lest he see that that was the last thing in the world she wanted from him. 'I... I just don't like to be touched.'

'I see ... I'm sorry.'

Of course he didn't see at all, which was just as well. The silence between them stretched to an uncomfortable minute and Bonnie at last turned back sufficiently to pick up her coffee-cup. But she did not return her eyes to his as she sipped, staring steadfastly over the rim of the cup at a spot to the right of his shoulder, and it was while she was determinedly studying the cars parked in the car park that her eyes landed on a highly familiar vehicle.

It wasn't a car but a combivan—a white combivan. And it belonged to Stan, her sister's husband.

But it wasn't Louise snuggled up next to him in the front cabin of the van, Bonnie quickly realised. Louise had light brown hair, not black. But it was Stan all right, Stan who was at that moment kissing the black-haired girl, kissing her as if there were no tomorrow.

Bonnie's cup froze mid-air between her mouth and the saucer; she was stunned by what she was seeing. Stan, whose twenty-year marriage to Louise she had always envied. Stan, who was a wonderful father to his three boys. Yet here he was, clearly involved with another woman, so involved that he would risk kissing her in a public car park in full view of anyone who might just happen to be there, like herself.

CHAPTER FIVE

JORDAN saw the shock till Bonnie's eyes, his own whipping round over his shoulder to see what could have caused such a look. All he could see of interest was a man and woman kissing in the front seat of a nearby combivan.

That had to be it. But was it the identity of the man or the woman that had shocked her?

By the time he turned back, she was on her feet and picking up her bag and keys. 'I need to get out of here,' was all she said, and was off, hurrying towards her car which was parked well out of sight of the combivan.

Jordan paid for the food and hurried after her, all the while trying to work out exactly what was going on. Maybe the angelic-looking Mrs Merrick wasn't as angelic as he'd deduced. Maybe she was exactly what that Neil fellow had implied she was in the first place. A right swinger, with men-friends all over the place. The term merry widow hadn't been coined for nothing.

By the time Jordan made it into the passenger seat of the green Falcon he'd invented an entire scenario. The man in the combivan was her latest lover and he was two-timing her. Why else would she be upset at seeing him kiss another woman?

'Mind telling me what that was all about?' he asked, his thoughts making his voice curt.

'Yes, I would,' she retorted just as curtly, and turned on the engine with shaking fingers. He reached over and turned it off again, bringing a sharp look of outrage to her face.

So! The increasingly enigmatic Mrs Merrick was not the type to countenance masterly behaviour in a man, not like Erica who was only too happy for him to do all the running, as well as make all the decisions. Suddenly he wasn't sure which attitude he preferred.

'I don't think you should drive when you're this upset,' he said firmly. 'Now who was that man, and why did seeing him with that woman distress you so much?'

He awaited her reply with baited breath, half wanting her to confirm his earlier guess, yet at the same time dreading it. What was it with this woman? What did he really want her to be? Saint or sinner?

'He's my brother-in-law,' she blurted out. 'And that girl with him wasn't my sister!' Her head dropped down into her hands with a groan. 'Poor Louise. Poor, poor Louise.'

And poor Jordan, he thought grimly as he stared over at her distraught figure. Hell, he was simply dying to reach over and draw her into his arms. But he knew he wouldn't stop at comforting her. If he had his way, he'd make that kissing couple in the car look innocent by comparison.

'I'm sorry,' he said brusquely.

'There's nothing for *you* to be sorry about,' she said agitatedly, her head lifting.

Jordan cringed inside. Little did she know. If she could see into his mind she might view his apology differently.

Her lovely face suddenly hardened with a bitter resolve. 'It's Stan who's going to be sorry,' she bit out. 'When Louise finds out what he's been up to, she'll boot him out the door so fast he won't know what hit him.'

'Good lord, you're not going to tell her, are you?' As much as he despised adultery and adulterers, there was nothing to be gained by making the innocent party aware of such goings-on.

'Too darn right I am.'

'Don't.'

'*Don't*?' She swivelled to face him in the confines of the car, and once again Jordan was in danger of losing control. God, but anger did become her, producing the same sort of physical symptoms as sexual arousal might. His mind reeled at the image of her lying naked beneath him in just such a fashion with her lovely pale cheeks all flushed and her green eyes glittering wildly.

'Why not?' she flung at him. 'Louise has a right to know what sort of man she's married to. What kind of a sister would I be if I didn't tell her?'

He dragged his mind out of the cesspool it was fast becoming with great difficulty. 'She won't thank you for it, I'll warrant,' he ground out. 'How long has she been married?'

'Twenty years this year. She's a good deal older than I am.'

'I presume she has children?'

'Three boys.'

'And you're going to destroy a twenty-year marriage on the strength of one stolen kiss?'

'That didn't look like one stolen kiss and you know it. It looked like a full-blooded affair!'

'Perhaps, but it's still assumption on your part. Even if your brother-in-law is having an affair, the odds are it'll peter out eventually. What your sister and her sons don't know won't hurt them, Bonnie. Think of their happiness, not revenge on your brother-in-law. I agree he's probably a rat, though even in that you shouldn't judge him too quickly. Maybe he and your sister have come to some arrangement regarding sex. Or maybe she suspects his philandering and is deliberately turning a blind eye. If you confront her with the truth, she might feel forced to do something about it when she doesn't really want to.'

She was wavering, he could see. But her original stance certainly showed him what she thought of unfaithful men in general.

'What if it doesn't peter out?' she agonised aloud. 'What if Stan's fallen in love with that girl and he's going to leave Louise?'

'That's quite a few "what if"s, Bonnie. Even if it was so, what point would there be in forewarning your sister? She'd only be miserable before she *had* to be miserable.'

'Yes…yes, you're probably right.' She dragged in then expelled a long, shuddering sigh. 'I should thank you, I suppose, for making me see reason.'

Jordan almost laughed. He wished someone could make him see reason. He knew it was pointless to keep on lusting after this woman. But that was exactly what he was doing. Madly. *Stupidly*!

Tonight could not come quickly enough. Come morning Erica would be officially his fiancée and this quite alien burst of uncontrollable desire would have been slated.

'It was the shock, you see,' the object of that desire was saying. 'I always thought Louise and Stan had the perfect marriage.'

'There's no such thing as a perfect marriage.'

'I'm beginning to appreciate that.'

Jordan heard something in her voice that set him thinking that maybe her marriage to that policeman had not exactly been a happy one, but when he started mulling over the ramifications of such a possibility he quickly pulled himself up short. Damn it all, it was nothing to him if her first husband had been the biggest louse of all time. He'd already made the decision not to follow through with anything where the lovely Mrs Merrick was concerned.

Forget about her, damn you!

'You feel fit to drive now?' he asked abruptly.

'What? Oh, yes, yes, of course. Gosh I've been raving on, haven't I? And I didn't pay my share of the dinner. Here, let me——'

'Don't worry about it,' he cut in forcefully. 'I can afford it. Let's get moving, shall we? Time is a-wasting, and I have an important appointment in Sydney this evening.'

The afternoon proved to be an intolerable strain for Bonnie. She couldn't stop thinking about Stan and that girl. Stan, whom she would have considered the last man on earth to have an affair.

Yet he was. No matter what Jordan said, she knew the evidence of her own eyes. Stan was sleeping with that girl. Why, he was so wrapped up in kissing her that the whole world could have blown up around him and he wouldn't have noticed.

Bonnie was worried sick that he might leave Louise, that he might want more than the occasional stolen moment with his lover. Oh, she wasn't naïve enough to think he'd fallen in love with that young chit. But men could be such fools where sex was concerned.

Dear heaven, Louise would be shattered if Stan left her. And so would the boys. Bonnie had agreed with Jordan that to tell her sister what she'd seen would achieve nothing, but it was simply awful knowing the truth and feeling totally helpless.

It was also awful trying to act normally as she showed Jordan around another half a dozen houses, when all she wanted was to go home and have a good cry.

By the time Bonnie pulled her car up next to Jordan's bronze sedan just after four-thirty, she was mentally and physically exhausted. Apart from her concerns over her sister's marriage, it was clear that her sickness over the weekend had weakened her normally robust constitution.

'Are you all right?' Jordan asked when she turned off the ignition with a ragged sigh.

She glanced over at him, a wan smile on her lips.

'I guess I'm a little tired,' she admitted. 'I was sick in bed with a virus over the weekend, and I think I'm suffering somewhat from the after-effects.'

His handsome face looked no less handsome under an exasperated expression. But seeing Stan with that girl had thankfully rendered her immune to his undeniable attractions. Nothing like witnessing a wonderful example of male infidelity to freeze even the remotest desire for the species.

'Why didn't you say you'd been ill?' he demanded impatiently. 'God, there I was, dragging you all over the countryside, making you show me every damned place on your books.' He stared hard into her face. 'You do look pale, come to think of it.'

Her laughter was slightly rattled under his close inspection. 'Yes, I know. And I have dark rings under my eyes too. But nothing that a spot of sun and a good night's sleep won't fix.'

'A good night's sleep,' he repeated slowly, unnerving her with the continuing intensity of his gaze. 'I could do with one of those...'

Suddenly, his eyes snapped away and he reached for the door-handle. 'Won't get one this way, however,' he muttered, opening the door and levering his tall frame out of the car. 'No, stay put,' he ordered brusquely when she went to climb out as well.

She looked over at where he was leaning down into the car with one hand on the roof and the other on the top of the door, the action having pulled open his suit jacket, revealing a broad chest and steely stomach. Bonnie found herself holding her breath, a sudden tightness in her chest warning her that she might not have become totally immune to this man after all. It was to be thanked he was safely engaged.

'You go home and go to bed,' he commanded. 'Now off you go. I'll lock the gates.'

'But I...I...'

'Don't argue with me, woman. You'll lose. Now go.'

'But what about Saturday?'

'What about it?'

'What...what time will you want me to show you and your fiancée those two houses you liked?'

For a split-second he said nothing, and she was sure he was going to tell her to forget the whole deal, that he had changed his mind about buying up here after all. In a way, she almost wished he would. Out of sight was out of mind...

The thought of never seeing him, however, brought a sharp dismay, which in turn brought panic. She didn't need this. Not now. Not ever!

'I could get one of the salesmen to show you around if you'd prefer,' she offered, her inner agitation making her voice curt.

A rather ruthless hardness entered his steady gaze. 'Now why would I want anyone other than you looking after me, Bonnie?'

Dear heaven but he could be an intimidating man when he wanted to be. Those eyes...so cold...so merciless.

Bonnie swallowed, determined not to be rattled. 'I was under the impression this morning that you preferred dealing with a man,' she said coolly.

'Really? How rude of me. Believe me when I say you're the one I want to handle me. No one else. Now go home. Come Saturday I want to see you looking bright-eyed and bushy-tailed. Shall we say eleven? Erica's not noted for her early risings.'

'Eleven would be fine.'

'Good. I'll see you at eleven, then. And Bonnie...'

'Y-yes?'

'Don't go saying anything to your sister.'

Bonnie blinked. She'd forgotten all about Stan and Louise for a moment. But now it all came back with a rush. Oh, God. Poor Louise.

'No. No, I won't,' she choked out. 'See you Saturday, then.'

He smiled then slammed the car door, leaning back against his sedan with his arms folded while she drove off. Her last sight of him in the rear-view mirror was him striding round the front of his car and stopping briefly to look up at the McClelland place, shaking his head as he did so. She too glanced at the house and was immediately bombarded by a whole host of emotions, not the least of which was a crushing sense of failure.

What was it she had done wrong? How had she let the old woman down? Surely she couldn't have expected her actually to sell Jordan her house? The idea was ludicrous. Perfectly ludicrous!

CHAPTER SIX

'AND where did you get to yesterday?' Daphne pounced first thing Tuesday morning. 'I was dying for you to come back.'

'Oh?' Bonnie tried to sound nonchalant. 'Why?'

'*Why*?' Daphne squeaked. 'Why do you think, silly?' A pitying glance followed. 'Really, Bonnie, I don't know what to make of you. You spent most of yesterday with the most gorgeous hunk of male flesh that I've ever seen and all you can do is look blank.'

'Oh, you mean Mr Vine-Hall. Yes, he's quite good-looking, I suppose, but I wouldn't have thought he was your type.' Daphne lived on a steady diet of young bronzed life-savers, of which the coast had a never-ending supply. 'Too old for one thing and not the sporty type. Here's the keys to the McClelland place. Want a cup of coffee? I'm about to get myself one.'

Daphne was not to be so easily side-tracked. 'What I want, Bonnie Merrick, is a complete run-down on you-know-who. I don't care if he's fifty and never seen a surfboard in his life. He's utterly gorgeous! Now ... is he married? What does he do for a crust? Is he going to buy a house up here? Come on, *give*.'

Bonnie sighed. After a sleepless night worrying about Stan and Louise's marriage—and some other equally disturbing things—she just wasn't up to an inquisition.

'Look, I don't know all that much,' she said wearily. 'He's a barrister, lives in Sydney, might be buying a weekender up here and is very, very engaged. He's

57

bringing his fiancée up to have a look at a couple of places this Saturday.'

'Oh, rats!' Daphne's pretty mouth formed into a sulky pout. 'All the good ones are always taken.' She mulled over the situation for a few brief seconds before brightening suddenly. 'What am I saying? Engaged is not married! Goodness, *married* is hardly married these days. An engagement is nothing. Tell me more. How old do you think he is? Thirty-five? More?'

'Thirty-six,' Bonnie said before she could think better of it. Her mind was still on Daphne's comments about engagements and marriage.

Daphne gave her a sharp look. 'I thought you said you didn't know much about him.'

'I don't really,' she hedged. 'Just the basics. Look, do you want a cup of coffee or not?'

'Nope. I'm off caffeine this week.'

Bonnie hurried off down the corridor towards the back room, noting on the way past that Neil's cubicle was empty. What a pity it wouldn't stay that way, she thought ruefully. She was momentarily tempted to tell Edgar what had happened the previous day, but she very quickly discarded that idea when the man himself joined her at the coffee-machine, a not too happy look on his face. Sales were down for their branch for the month, and it was hardly the time to stir up trouble. No, she would just have to handle Neil by herself.

'Didn't see much of you yesterday,' Edgar said. 'Where did you get to?'

Bonnie told him all about her day showing Jordan around and made it sound as if she had a sure sale in the bag. It brightened the boss up no end.

'That's great, Bonnie. Did you get a chance to have a look at the McClelland place?'

'Yes, I did as a matter of fact, and it's going to be really hard to sell.'

Edgar groaned. 'Tell me something I don't know already.'

'Actually, I rather liked the place myself,' she confessed. 'It has character.'

'Then why don't *you* buy it?' he quipped drily as he stalked off to his office, coffee in hand.

Bonnie stared after him for a moment, his suggestion seizing her brain—*and* her heart. Immediately, she began shaking her head in denial of the impulse. No, she couldn't. It was a crazy idea. Crazy! For one thing, it was too expensive. And too isolated, and too darned spooky. Besides, she already owned a house. She didn't need another.

Turning back to the coffee-machine, she put the insane notion firmly to one side and got on with making herself an adrenalin boost. God knew she needed it after the horrible night she'd had.

'If you tell me you unloaded that white elephant on to your pin-striped client of yesterday,' Neil said from just behind her shoulder, 'then I'll get down on this floor and kiss your feet! Frankly, I'll kiss your feet if you unloaded *anything* on to him.'

Bonnie's chest tightened as she struggled to keep her temper.

'Well?' Neil goaded. 'Cat got your tongue or something? What happened? Didn't you find favour with his Lordship or something? Don't tell me he wasn't smitten by your charms like every other male within smelling distance.'

Bonnie's empty hand curled into an angry fist. If she were a man, she'd sock him one right in that supercilious mouth of his. Instead, she gradually relaxed her fingers, scooped in a steadying breath and did her best to keep her cool.

'I think, Neil,' she said firmly as she turned from the coffee-machine to face him, 'that we should have a little talk.'

'Really? What about?'

'About what you said yesterday, for one thing.'

'Oh, yeah? Like what specifically? I said a lot of things yesterday.'

Bonnie was surprised to see that he was looking a little rattled, an almost guilty flush staining his cheekbones.

'You know darned well what I'm talking about, Neil. Even before you said what you said about me and Edgar, you'd been making it difficult for us to work amicably together. All those snide remarks and looks. And all because I won't go out with you. For a highly intelligent man, don't you think you're acting pretty stupidly?'

Bonnie watched as Neil struggled over whether to respond to her insult or her flattery. He *wasn't* an overly intelligent man. Jordan made him look moronic by comparison. But that didn't mean he didn't fancy himself the smartest young stud on the Central Coast.

'I am not sleeping with Edgar,' she swept on before he came to a decision. 'I'm not sleeping with any man. Neither was I an unfaithful wife. Keith was a very jealous and possessive husband and used to imagine all sorts of things. I loved my husband, Neil,' she lied. 'His death devastated me and I'm simply not ready for a new involvement just yet. Please stop taking my refusing your invitations as a personal insult. There's nothing personal in it. I think you're a very attractive man, and if I wanted a relationship with anyone I'm sure you would be high on my list. But I don't, and that's that. I'm sorry.'

Yes, she thought bitterly. Damned sorry that I have to demean myself like this just to make life bearable.

Neil was staring at her with the most odd look on his face—a mixture of surprise and relief. 'For a moment there I thought...' he began, then cleared his throat. 'Look, Bonnie, I'm sorry too,' he startled her by saying. 'I guess I'm not used to females who look like you do not being interested in—er—you know. But be warned. I might still ask you out occasionally, and who knows? One day, when you're fed up with your own company at night, you might say yes.'

With that, he smiled, and in truth it was a very attractive smile. Why, then, did it leave her cold, when Jordan's smile sent her heart pounding and her nerve-endings jangling? It was most peculiar.

'You didn't close a sale yesterday, then?' he asked.

'No, though Mr Vine-Hall is supposed to be coming back on Saturday with his fiancée...'

'He probably won't even turn up,' Neil remarked as he wandered off. 'People just say that.'

In a way, Bonnie hoped Neil was right. As much as one part of her said she should be grateful to find out she was still a normal woman with normal desires—a lot of women wouldn't have been after what she'd been through with Keith—she was still perturbed by her on-going sexual awareness of Jordan.

Her greatest fear since Keith was that some day she might fall in love with another wickedly handsome man who would enslave her senses with his sexual expertise, then slowly use his power over her emotions and body to control and undermine her entire self.

Not that she had anything to worry about where Jordan was concerned. There was little risk of them ever becoming intimately involved. Their relationship—such as it was—was strictly business, the chemistry Bonnie felt in his presence all one-sided.

Or was it? she frowned. Hadn't there been the odd moment or two when she'd been aware of something coming from Jordan, an intensity that might have been desire? Bonnie knew full well that a lot of men found her sexually attractive despite her ongoing attempts to play down her physical attributes. She also knew that some men forgot all about right or wrong when it came to pursuing their carnal desires. Just look at Stan.

What if Jordan was just such a man? What if he decided to forget he was a gentleman—*and* engaged—and make a pass at her? How would she react?

Bonnie's frown deepened, especially when just thinking about such a possibility sent a tiny shiver of unbidden excitement racing through her.

Her stomach contracted, self-disgust bringing a grimace of distaste to her lips. So that was the lie of the land, was it? She was still weak in that regard. Wickedly, pathetically weak.

Bonnie grimaced. If that was the case she would have to be very careful around Jordan. Very, very careful. Hopefully, Neil's prognostication about Jordan showing up would prove to be right. It would be much better all round if he stayed well away from her.

But some inner instinct told her he would show up on Saturday. Jordan was not a man who just said things. He followed through.

No. Come Saturday morning he would roll up here right on eleven. There was no doubt about it in her mind. All she could do to protect her peace of mind was to prepare herself mentally, emotionally and physically for a very difficult day.

*   *   *

Bonnie's watch showed eight minutes to eleven when she glanced at it for the umpteenth time.

She was nervous. Horribly nervous. Which dismayed her. She'd felt perfectly in control when she'd arrived this morning, but as the minutes had ticked away so had her composure.

She was about to get up from her desk and walk down the back of the office when her telephone buzzed.

Oh, please, she prayed as she reached to pick it up. Please let that be Jordan saying he's changed his mind and won't be coming.

'Mrs Merrick,' she answered, nerves making her voice crisp.

'Goodness, don't you sound efficient?'

'Oh, Louise, it's *you*!'

'Yes, it's me, your ever-loving sister. I'm still alive, and so, it seems, are you. So why haven't I heard from you lately?'

'I—er—I've been pretty busy.'

'With work, I suppose,' Louise said drily.

'Yes.'

'Pity... I was rather hoping your silence meant you'd found yourself a man at long last.'

Bonnie swallowed. Said nothing.

'OK, I get the message. I promise not to nag. But you can't grieve for Keith for the rest of your life.'

Bonnie winced. She'd never confided the horrors of her marriage to Louise, either before or after Keith's death. She'd been too ashamed.

'Life goes on,' Louise was saying. 'And there are still plenty of other nice men out there. I married one, didn't I?'

Bonnie's mind filled with a mental image of Stan and that girl kissing, and her insides tightened.

Louise sighed. 'I can see I'm wasting my breath. Look, the main reason I called was to see if you'd like to come over for a few hours tonight. Stan's going to Sydney this afternoon with a mate to watch a day-night cricket match and won't be home till well after midnight. I'm going to be all alone.'

Bonnie smothered the urge to comment on Stan's sudden interest in cricket. He'd always said he hated watching cricket, complaining it was as boring as watching grass grow.

'Oh?' she said instead. 'Where are the boys going to be?'

'Peter's away on a school camping excursion, Mikey's staying the night with his best friend, and Tom's off to a disco with his latest girl. He's nearly eighteen, you know.'

'Yes, I know.'

'Well, what do you say? Can you come?'

'Yes, of course. I'd love to.'

'Great! I'll make your favourite spaghetti bolognese.'

Bonnie smiled. 'Thanks, Mum.'

Louise laughed. 'I do still mother you, don't I? Can't seem to throw away the habit.'

Louise had always been like a second mother to Bonnie. In truth, their own mother hadn't been much of a parent, living in a kind of dream world after their father had died of a stroke when Bonnie was only two. She'd been sickly too, suffering from a wide variety of ailments which the doctors had told her two daughters were all psychosomatic. So Bonnie and Louise had been very shocked when their mother had passed away in her sleep the year Bonnie was to sit for her Higher School Certificate.

Which might have explained why Bonnie hadn't exactly passed with flying honours. After her mother's death she'd gone to live with Louise and Stan at Morriset while she did a secretarial course at Wyong Tech.

But she'd hated living away from the beach, so as soon as she'd finished her course she'd taken a job as a receptionist in one of the many real-estate offices around Blackrock Beach—not Coastal Properties—then moved into a flat there with some friends. A week later she had met Keith, and started on the pathway to hell...

'I promise I won't nag you, love,' Louise added, Bonnie catching the slightly plaintive note in her voice. Clearly she was desperate for some company.

'I'll remind you you said that,' Bonnie teased gently. 'Look, Louise, I must go. I have an important client who's just walked in and he's bound to get testy if I don't jump and dance attendance on him straight away.'

'Yuck, he sounds revolting. I couldn't do your job for love nor money. I'll see you around six, then?'

'Yes, around then. Bye for now.'

'Bye.'

Bonnie hung up, her mouth dry, her pulse racing. She could see Jordan through the glass partition of her cubicle, and he was looking anything but revolting. Dressed in a pair of black trousers and a short-sleeved black silk shirt, left open at the neck, he exuded a subtle sexiness which had Bonnie's heart thudding, even from the safety of distance. She watched him step up to the reception desk, all panther-like elegance, even his slightly wind-blown hair not lessening his air of cool sophistication. He simply combed the errant waves back into place with splayed fingers, at the same time addressing a fatuous-faced Daphne in smoothly unhurried tones.

'Good morning. Mrs Merrick is expecting me. Could you please inform her I've arrived?'

Bonnie rose from her desk immediately, knowing that any delay would only make her more nervous, as well as take the initiative away from her. She had a certain reputation for her own cool composure around the office and had no intention of spoiling that in front of Daphne.

Or Jordan.

Especially in front of Jordan, she vowed staunchly.

Plastering a polite smile on her face, she walked along the corridor towards the reception area, the smile becoming a little stiff once she passed the last desk and moved into full view, especially when Jordan turned and those intense black eyes of his washed over her from top to toe. His expression seemed quite bland and expressionless, but something—a momentary glitter in those dark depths perhaps?—warned her that he was not indifferent to how she looked.

Bonnie resisted the impulse to glance down at her clothes and check that nothing about her appearance was in any way provocative. For she knew there wasn't. The buttercup-yellow shirtwaister she was wearing was very simple and modest, of sufficient size to skim, not hug her figure, with stitched-down pockets covering her breasts, no belt pulling in her tiny waist, the hem length reaching her knees. It had plain white buttons down the front, all of them done up, her only concession to the heat of the day being no stockings and open-toed white sandals on her feet.

Her make-up was at a minimum, her hair caught back with a yellow scarf. No earrings swung from her lobes. No perfume wafted from her skin. No other jewellery twinkled or clinked. She was without adornment. She was, she thought, as plain as possible. He had no *right* to find her attractive.

She desperately wanted to stamp her foot in frustration. Instead, she crossed those last few steps between them, her voice crisp and cool.

'You're very punctual.'

'I try to be,' came his rather curt reply, his eyes lifting back to hers. 'Can you come straight away? I have my car parked in a five-minute spot.'

'I'll just get my car keys and bag.'

When she turned to walk briskly back to her desk, Jordan only just resisted expelling an exasperated sigh. Aware of the receptionist staring at him, he dragged his gaze away from Bonnie Merrick's oh, so watchable behind, willed his body from imminent arousal to an iron-clad repose, then spun and strode outside to wait for her on the pavement. Only then, unobserved, did he allow himself a ragged exhalation.

What the hell was he doing here? Why was he putting himself through this torment, prolonging the pain?

He'd discovered last Monday night that he'd been dead wrong calling what he felt for her just a temporary sexual aberration due to frustration. The truth had hit him when he'd tried to take Erica to bed and found that he couldn't.

'Well, not *couldn't* exactly. He could have, but only by closing his eyes and pretending the body beneath him was none other than Mrs Bonnie Merrick.

The idea had repulsed him, and he'd immediately stopped the futile lovemaking, excusing himself by saying he was too tired to do justice to the act. Erica's understanding had irritated him so much that his earlier resolve to ask her to marry him that night had also flown out the window. Unfortunately, he'd already told her about the beach-house he wanted to buy, plus his plan to bring her up on the weekend, and she'd jumped at the idea, thinking, no doubt, that this meant he was on the verge of proposing.

A deep and dark inner instinct had warned him all week to ring up and cancel the appointment. But his ego had refused to let him and now here he was, faced with the stupidity of his arrogant conclusion that this time

Bonnie Merrick in the flesh would have no effect on him
at all other than inspiring a superficial admiration of her
physical beauty. Forewarned was forearmed, he'd told
himself. There would be no lightning strike of fierce
desire a second time, no mad urge to throw conscience
to the winds and do anything—*anything*—to have her.

He'd been wrong.

She came through the doorway to join him, stepping
into the sunlight like a golden angel. It was ironic, he
thought testily, that such an exquisitely celestial creature
should be consigning his body—and maybe his soul—
to hell.

If he gave in to temptation, that was. But he had no
intention of doing that!

The only course of action was to keep this visit as
short as possible, buy the first house Erica liked, then
go back to Sydney and try to forget the female. Jordan
wanted nothing to do with a woman who could make
him lose all common sense and control. Maybe he would
have understood himself better if their passion had been
mutual. But there had not been even a hint of flirtation
in her manner towards him so far, and she'd had plenty
of opportunity.

God knew what would have happened if she had given
him the eye. He didn't like to think about it!

'My car is over there,' he said, pointing across the
main street to the sleek sedan parked in front of the surf
club. Bonnie caught a glimpse of blonde hair in the
passenger seat before looking back at Jordan.

'Mine's behind the office. It won't take me a minute
to fetch it. I'll slow down as I pass you and you can pull
out behind me. I think we should go to see the house at
Cairncross Bay first, since you're pointed that way.'

'Which one was that?'

'The white split-level one on the side of a hill. You liked the balconies, remember? And the view.'

'Yes, it was the better of the two. We'll definitely look at it first and if Erica likes it we won't need to see the other one. We can come straight back here and I'll sign on the dotted line.'

Bonnie gasped at his decisiveness. 'Just like that?'

'I don't have a lot of time. I have to be back in Sydney by two, which gives us an hour and a half at most.'

Bonnie should have been relieved, or even ecstatic, that she could dispense with the object of her unease, plus wrap up a sale, all within such a short space of time. But she wasn't, which was quite perverse of her.

Dear God, had her marriage to Keith turned her into some kind of a masochist?

'We'd better get a move on, then,' she said with a fixed smile on her face. 'Keep an eye out for my car. You know the one. It's a green Falcon.'

Two minutes later the bronze sedan slid into place behind her and they proceeded at a sedate speed round the curving roads that hugged the coastline and took them to Cairncross Bay.

Bonnie had to keep resisting the urge to look in the rear-view mirror, telling herself not to care what Jordan's fiancée looked like. Erica was as irrelevant to her life as Jordan would be after today. All she should be caring about at this point in time was the lovely commission she was about to make.

So why was she even now giving in to temptation and looking in that damned mirror, searching to see if the sleekly beautiful blonde hair she had sighted back at Blackrock Beach was matched by a sleekly beautiful face?

It didn't take more than a moment's glance to have her suspicion confirmed.

Bonnie wrenched her eyes away and back on to the road ahead, which was just as well since they were about to go round a hairpin bend. OK, so Erica had a great face. A face was just a face. Maybe she wouldn't have such a great figure. Maybe she'd be bottom-heavy, with no bust, thick ankles and dimpled thighs.

A burst of laughter bubbled up in Bonnie's throat. I'm going mad, she decided. Quite mad. Oh, lord, please let the next hour and a half fly. I don't think I can take much more of this!

CHAPTER SEVEN

THE hill leading up to the house at Cairncross Bay was not for the faint-hearted. Bonnie carefully directed her Falcon into the kerb alongside the 'FOR SALE' sign, turned off the engine and yanked on the handbrake as hard as she could. Jordan went past, did a U-turn and parked opposite with his car facing downhill.

Their eyes met as they both alighted, Bonnie deliberately not sending even a polite smile across at him. Smiles, she'd often found, even the most innocuous ones, could be misinterpreted.

Not that her unsmiling face seemed to bother him, since he immediately looked away and started striding round to the passenger side of the car.

Her earlier concern that Jordan might be impelled to try his hand at seducing her was beginning to feel ridiculous. There was not a hint of flirtation in his demeanour today. Any man planning on making some sort of pass at some stage would have taken advantage of the time he was alone with her outside the office, or at least held her eyes for more than a split-second.

The realisation that Jordan was not smitten by her charms, as Neil had nastily suggested the other day, should have brought relief. Instead, she felt almost put out.

Her irritation soared as she watched Jordan open the passenger door, take his fiancée's hand and genteelly draw her on to her feet. He hadn't done the same for her the other day. Not once.

71

Seeing Jordan dance such chivalrous attendance on his fiancée brought a sharp stab of emotion Bonnie refused to recognise as jealousy. Surely it had to be simply annoyance at witnessing such an outdated custom? What modern, healthy young woman would want that kind of treatment anyway, as though she were an incompetent or an invalid, incapable of getting out of a silly car?

Not me, she thought defiantly. I'm my own person now and I aim to stay that way. I don't want any man treating me like some delicate piece of porcelain. It's all a con anyway. They do nice things at first, pretending they care about you, telling you they love you. But it's all a ploy, a ploy to get you into their bed and under their thumb. And then they begin to change, and... and...

A shudder ran through her as she stepped up on to the pavement. It was good to remember. Very good. It gave her the strength to ignore all the silly weak feelings she kept having. Straightening her shoulders, she turned and watched Jordan steer his beloved Erica across the road, her self-lecture almost making her see irony in the situation.

As if such a man would look twice at her anyway, when he had a creature like that on his arm, and in his bed.

Bonnie's mouth tipped up at one corner in a small, self-mocking smile. Try as she might, she could not find one single physical flaw in the woman. Dressed in a cool blue suit and pearls, she was a young Grace Kelly reincarnated, her figure having the same classic perfection as her face, her fair hair sleek and silky in a shoulder-length bob.

The only minor fault Bonnie could come up with was a slightly vacuous expression in her big baby-blue eyes. If she didn't know better, she might think the girl was

lacking in intelligence. Or maybe she was just very prac-
tised at looking like that. Some women seemed to think
playing dumb was the way to go.

'This is Mrs Merrick,' Jordan introduced her.

'How do you do, Mrs Merrick?' Erica said sweetly,
though the ingenuous blue gaze did flash for a moment.
'Jordan, you bad man,' his fiancée went on, sending an
adoringly teasing look up at him. 'You didn't tell me
Mrs Merrick was so ravishingly beautiful. And to think
you spent most of last Monday with her! Just as well
she's a safely married woman or I might be jealous.'

Bonnie frowned. Clearly Jordan had not mentioned
she was a widow, and to say as much at this juncture
could be awkward. Jordan caught her eye and managed
to convey with a single steely glance that she should keep
quiet on the subject. His not calling her Bonnie hadn't
escaped her either, and she concluded that Erica was
perhaps of a jealous nature.

No doubt being engaged to a man as impressive as
Jordan could give rise to some worries. Women would
be throwing themselves at him all the time. Just look at
Daphne this morning, gushing and gawking. The thought
made Bonnie all the more determined to remain totally
cool in his presence. At least when all this was over her
pride would remain intact, even if not her total peace of
mind.

'Shall we go inside?' she suggested smoothly. 'You did
say you hadn't much time...'

Half an hour later they were standing on the balcony
of the second house, this one several miles away at
Wamberal, Jordan having decided against the first house
because of several nit-picking reasons he hadn't mentioned the other day. Now, once again, he seemed to be
finding faults. Thankfully, the house was unoccupied,

so there was no owner hovering who might take offence at his comments.

'There isn't a suitable room for my study,' he complained.

'But what do you want a study for, darling?' Erica queried. 'You won't want to work on the odd weekend you spend up here, surely?'

'Actually, I wanted this place as more than a weekender. I might pop up during the week sometimes.'

Erica looked taken aback, but was obviously not given to arguing with Jordan over anything he wanted to do. She tucked her arm more tightly through his and gave him another of her simpering smiles. 'Whatever you say, darling. Maybe Mrs Merrick has some other place on her books which already has a study set up in it.'

'Have you?' he asked brusquely.

'Several. But you've already seen them and didn't like any. The only place which has what I think would be the perfect room for you you refused to really look at.'

His frown was full of puzzlement. 'What place? I don't recall refusing to look at any place last Monday. Lord, you don't mean that first old dump, do you? You can't seriously think I would consider buying *that* place!'

'I don't think you gave it a chance,' Bonnie returned with cool reason. 'Yes, it *is* old and might look like a dump...on the surface. But it's quite solid and, with a bit of money spent on it, would look very different indeed. It's going remarkably cheap for where it is and the amount of land it's sitting on. There'll be a splendid view of the ocean once some selected scrub and trees have been removed, and I'm told there's a trail down the cliff to a private cove suitable for swimming. But on top of all that it has a charming library which is quiet and peaceful and absolutely perfect for a writer's den.'

'A writer!' Erica exclaimed, somewhat scornfully. 'Jordan's not a *writer*. Heavens to Betsy! Tell her, darling. Tell her what you are. Goodness, she actually thinks you're a writer,' she finished with a droll laugh.

Bonnie saw the muscles stiffen in his jaw, saw the intense irritation in his eyes. She felt irritation herself. No wonder he'd kept his writing a secret, if his nearest and dearest had this attitude. What on earth was wrong with being a writer? Maybe it didn't rank with being a queen's counsel but it was still an honest profession.

'I've been doing some writing lately, Erica,' he confessed ruefully. 'And I aim to do some more.'

'But... but...'

'I'll tell you about it later,' he snapped. 'Meanwhile, I think I'll go have a look at this library.'

Erica's face did not look quite so lovely with her mouth agape. After a few seconds her mouth snapped shut, after which she threw Bonnie a witheringly sour look. But she made no further reproof to Jordan. Not a word.

Bonnie felt some pity for her. She'd done the same thing herself a million times while married to Keith: kept her mouth shut when she'd ached to speak out, to argue, to voice an opinion. Her reason for keeping silent had been the same at first. Fear of losing her man. But in the end it had been very different.

It was obvious that the girl thought this was how you kept such a man—by being a mealy-mouthed clinging vine, letting him have his way all the time, being submissive and fawning, never rocking the boat.

Bonnie wanted to tell her she was wrong, that that was the way to failure and self-destruction. But how could she? It was none of her business. Erica wouldn't listen anyway. What woman did when she was in love?

But was Erica really in love with Jordan? Bonnie wondered as she trailed after them out of the house.

Maybe what she was in love with was the life she could live as Jordan's wife. Some women craved social position and material success so much that they were prepared to do anything to achieve that end.

Not that it would be any great hardship being Jordan's wife. Bonnie could think of worse fates.

Such thinking brought her up with a jolt. Till today, the idea of being *anyone's* wife had filled her with horror. Yet now she had to admit that the idea of seeing Jordan across the breakfast-table every morning was not without its attractions, be they mostly what might have transpired the night before.

Bonnie smothered a sigh. Back to sex again. Truly, she was incorrigibly stupid. Good sex did not a good marriage make. Hadn't she learnt that lesson yet? She and Keith had been very happy in bed at first. Too happy, as it turned out.

'Mrs Merrick? Jordan's talking to you.'

Bonnie blinked, only then aware that they were out on the pavement. She produced a polite smile for Erica, who seemed shocked that anyone would dare not hang on her beloved's every word. 'Sorry,' she said lightly. 'I was thinking.'

'A dangerous occupation,' Jordan drawled.

She turned to look at him and their eyes locked, his expression totally unreadable yet managing to project an insidiously seductive intimacy. Bonnie gulped down the sudden thickness in her throat, willing herself to remain calm. She had to be imagining things, of course, her thoughts of a moment ago feeding wild fantasies into her head. He wasn't flirting with her. One only had to glance Erica's way to see that. She wouldn't be looking so unconcerned if her man's eyes were really straying. He'd merely delivered an off-the-cuff comment, accompanied by a perfectly normal look.

'I was saying that I'd better still follow you,' he elaborated, his tone nonchalant. 'I know I've been there before but that place isn't easy to find.'

'True,' Bonnie agreed, amazed at how totally in control she sounded when inside she was a mess. 'I'll have to stop briefly on the way through Blackrock Beach and pick up the keys.'

'Fine. Let's go, then. Time and tide waits for no man.'

Being alone in the car as she drove to the McClelland house was a godsend to Bonnie. She was able to gather herself totally, put her thoughts and feelings into perspective. She had been over-reacting badly to the realisation that she could still be sexually attracted to a man.

Though to be fair to herself she had to admit that Jordan wasn't any old man. He was an exceptionally impressive male, not at all run-of-the-mill. As she'd already noted, even Daphne had gone ape over him. To castigate herself unduly for the way he'd been making her feel was most unfair to herself.

By the time she turned down the dirt road, her outward composure was no longer a sham, but reality, achieved by reaffirming to herself that she was a mature, confident woman nowadays, quite capable of handling herself in any situation, even an awkward case of one-sided lust.

Once her thoughts and feelings were under control, she swung her mind on to the job in hand, which was selling Jordan the McClelland place. Who knew? Maybe, if he spent a little more time in the house, especially in the library, he might see what *she* saw. As for Erica...well, she would go along with whatever Jordan decided. That much was patently clear. It was up to Bonnie to convince him that with a fresh coat of paint, a spot of gardening and a smattering of refurbishing the old house would be a changed sight, not to mention quite a good investment at the price. Perhaps, though, she wouldn't mention just yet that the house and land had to remain intact forever, with the land never being subdivided.

Bonnie felt a surge of optimism. What a feather in her cap it would be if she did sell the McClelland place! And to Jordan Vine-Hall, of all people.

Yet it would be just perfect for him. She *felt* it. And it wasn't as though he didn't have enough money to do it up properly. She was sure Mrs McClelland would like seeing the place all painted and sparkling as well.

Bonnie pulled herself up short at this last thought. The woman was dead! She could no longer feel pleasure or pain. She couldn't care who bought the house, who lived in it or what they did with it. It was unnerving to keep entertaining such ridiculous notions and Bonnie vowed to stop them. Right now!

Coming to a halt in front of the gates, she climbed out and unlocked them, throwing the decrepit and creepy old building a reproachful look as she pushed them, creaking, open. 'Try to look inviting, will you?' she muttered under her breath.

The realisation that she'd now started talking to the darned place sent laughter bubbling from her throat. She was still chuckling when she returned to the car, her laughter dying when she caught a glimpse of the two people sitting in the car right behind her. Erica's face carried a disgusted expression, while Jordan's wasn't much better.

Any faint hope that he might actually buy the house faded. Oh, well . . . it had been worth a try.

With a sigh, she climbed back in behind the wheel and drove up to park near the front steps. Jordan once again turned his car around so that he was facing the gateway, as though anxious to make a speedy exit. She was half expecting him to not even get out, but he did. Not with fiancée in tow, however.

'Erica says if I buy this place I've lost my mind,' he said on joining her at the base of the steps. 'And I have to agree with her. But curiosity has got the better of me.'

Bonnie's spirits bucked up a bit at this comment. Maybe a little of the house's charm had rubbed off on him the other day without him realising it. 'You might be pleasantly surprised,' she said as they walked up to the front door together and she inserted the key. 'This house has a way of getting to people.'

His laugh was quite dry. 'I'll blame it on the house, then, shall I?'

'Blame what?'

'Curiosity killed the cat, my dear Bonnie,' he said cryptically.

'But I'm not a cat,' she replied, shaken by her response to his using her first name again, especially with the 'my dear' attached.

All her earlier worries and fears came back with a rush, and along with them a strong feeling of premonition. What was it telling her? *Not* to go into the house alone with Jordan? Or was it just the opposite...compelling her practically to drag him inside post-haste?

'We must hurry.'

She stared at him, because while they were *his* words *she* had been thinking them.

'Yes,' she said, her voice oddly husky.

She went in first, knowing he was right behind her, though she never once glanced over her shoulder. Opening the door on her immediate right, she switched on the light then stepped back to wave him inside. She couldn't bring herself to look at him as he moved past her and into the library, something warning her that to do so would be dangerous. But when the seconds ticked away and nothing was said, she was driven to look up.

He was moving slowly around the room, touching things lightly as he went. The back of a chair, the fold of a curtain, a book on a shelf. She could feel him absorbing the atmosphere which had struck her when she'd first come into this house last Monday. The welcoming warmth, the cosiness, the certainty that it had once been a happy house, full of love and good vibes.

Suddenly, he stopped moving, his back to her, his shoulders stiffening. He seemed to be staring across at the armchair in the corner by the window, the one next to the old standard lamp. It had clearly been someone's reading chair, with a small side-table next to it and an ancient footstool not far away. A man's chair, Bonnie fancied. Maybe it was where old Mrs McClelland's husband used to sit.

When Jordan finally moved, he walked across and lowered himself into that same chair, propping his feet up on the footstool, his head tipping back against the worn head-rest, his eyes shutting on a weary, whispery sigh. Finally, he was perfectly still, perfectly, perfectly still. He might have been dead except for the faint rise and fall of his chest.

Bonnie's breath caught in her throat when she felt a chilly little breeze whisper around her legs. Of course it was probably only a draught from the front door, which she hadn't closed after them. But when she glanced back over her shoulder she was shocked to see that the front door was, in fact, shut. Her head whipped back round to stare at Jordan, sitting in that chair, and a shiver ran down her spine. She opened her mouth to say something but no words came out. Her brain willed her legs to move but they refused. All she could do was stare over at Jordan's silent and still form.

Gradually—almost as though in slow motion—his dark eyes opened, but their usual sharpness was dimmed, a dream-like expression clouding them. They drifted around the room then over to where she remained standing like a statue in the doorway. Ever so slowly his mouth curved back into a sensuously bewitching smile.

'Aren't you supposed to bring me my pipe and slippers?'

The words seem to come from some far-off place, not Jordan's lips. Bonnie found herself crossing the room, but the legs that carried her did not feel like her own. It was as if she were still standing near the doorway watching two strangers enact a scene from a play. She somehow reached the chair, her fingers trance-like as they moved to place the imaginary pipe on the table beside him. His eyes held her, seemed to draw her, and she sank to the floor at his knees, one hand coming to rest on his thigh.

'There you are, darling,' she murmured softly, and her hand started travelling slowly upwards.

'Jordan! Oh, Jord-an!'

At the sound of Erica's voice, Bonnie's hand whipped from Jordan's leg and she jumped to her feet. When she looked back down at him he was staring up at her, his expression stunned.

'Jordan, darling,' Erica's voice came again, louder this time. 'It's getting late. Didn't you say you had to be back in Sydney by two?'

Still Jordan neither spoke nor moved. He seemed pole-axed by the incident. Bonnie took the initiative, masking her inner turmoil behind a falsely cool façade. 'Your fiancée's calling you,' she said, her voice curiously flat.

Jordan blinked, then rose, frowning now as he yelled, 'Coming!' to the woman outside.

'So what do you think?' Bonnie asked him, shocking herself with her casual demeanour. 'Are you interested?'

'I'm not sure,' came his still frowning reply. 'I'll have to give the matter some further thought.'

'It's a bargain at the price, you know,' she pointed out, desperate to keep talking in a normal fashion. Dear God, what must he be thinking?

'I'm sure it is,' came his measured reply.

'You seemed to like this room. It's very relaxing, isn't it?'

'It certainly has something...'

She tried a smile. 'I did say the house had a way of getting to you. Some people say it's haunted.'

'I don't believe in ghosts,' he said with an abrupt coldness. 'I don't believe in anything like that. Look, I'll be in touch. I don't have any more time right now. No, don't bother to see me out. I know the way.' And he whirled and stalked from the room.

Bonnie stared after him, flinching when she heard his car start up and accelerate away.

'Oh, great,' she groaned aloud. 'Just great.'

What a fiasco! Lord knew what he'd thought when she'd called him darling and started sliding her hand up his thigh. She hardly knew what to think of it herself!

For it hadn't been *her* doing it. She was sure of that. It had been someone else, some force, some spirit directing her movements, making her say and do things that she would never have done of her own accord.

And now...now Jordan would not be back. He would not buy this house from her, or any other house for that matter!

Humiliation heated her blood, and her temper. She glared around the room, striding out into the hallway and up the stairs, flinging open the door of the nursery.

'Well, I *do* believe in ghosts. *Now*,'' she thundered, not at all afraid, only furious. 'And I won't tolerate being possessed. Do you hear me?'

Her voice echoed in the house but naturally there was no answer. Only an empty silence. Whatever presence—or presences—had directed her actions this afternoon, it was lying quiet now that Jordan had left. But it was still there, waiting. Yes, there was definitely a waiting within these walls. A waiting and a wanting. She had sensed it before.

Maybe if the ghost's intentions were clear she wouldn't have minded. But she couldn't tolerate being totally in the dark, the not knowing, the feeling that she was a pawn in some supernatural game she had no knowledge of. If old Mrs McClelland wanted something of her then let her spirit appear and tell her straight out what it was she wanted.

Which, of course, was not going to happen! Whatever that wicked old woman had on the agenda for her house was a secret, a dark and devious secret which mere mortals were not privy to. They were simply pawns, to be moved about at will, with no respect for *their* will.

'Well, you won't be moving *me* about again!' she warned. 'Because I'm not coming back here. Not ever. No way!'

With that Bonnie spun on her heel and stormed from the room, slamming the door shut behind her. Stomping down the stairs, she muttered away to herself quite savagely. If there was one thing she could not bear these days it was anyone—even a ghost!—usurping her right to control her own life. She'd fought her way back from the brink of total mush to at least a respectable amount of confidence and self-determination and she was damned if she was going to let some stupid sneaky spectre undermine that.

She stepped out on to the veranda, shutting and locking the door behind her quite firmly.

'Goodbye, Mrs McClelland!' she shouted. 'Goodbye, house! Work your monstrous magic on some other unsuspecting soul in future because it's *not* going to be *me*.'

CHAPTER EIGHT

'You're in a strange mood tonight.'

'Oh?' Bonnie looked up from where she was setting the table. Louise was standing at the kitchen counter, serving up the spaghetti. 'In what way do you mean?'

'You're all uptight, which isn't like you at all. Certainly not over the last couple of years. You've become quite the career-girl, so cool and competent, nothing at all like the rather shy, introverted girl you once were.'

'I guess I am a bit uptight,' Bonnie admitted with a sigh.

'Really? What on earth about?'

Bonnie was tempted to tell her everything that had happened this week. Everything, that was, except seeing Stan with that girl.

There had been a time, during her growing-up years, when Louise had filled the role of adviser and confidante, their mother being too vague to be of any real help to the young teenaged Bonnie. But after her marriage to Keith she'd gradually stopped telling her sister her worries, especially when Keith had started intimidating her both physically and emotionally. Frankly, by then Bonnie had begun to realise that Louise was rather naïve in matters of men, and life, and even sex. She was also very shockable. Bonnie knew her sister would have died if she'd told her what had been happening in her marriage.

Bonnie realised it was too late to tell her everything now. It was all too complicated and too...weird. Especially what had happened to her today. Louise would

scoff at any talk of ghosts. She was even more of a dis-
believer in the supernatural than Bonnie used to be. No,
she couldn't possibly tell her everything.

But she would have to tell her *something*.

'I—er—I've been having some problems at work,' she
said by way of excuse.

'What kind of problems?'

Bonnie sighed. She wished she hadn't started this.
'With one of the men. He keeps asking me out and I
keep telling him no. He's beginning to get nasty about
it.

'What's he like?'

'All beauty and no brains.'

'Hmm. Doesn't sound much different to Keith, then,
does he?'

Bonnie's eyes blinked wide. 'I thought you *liked* Keith.'

Louise pulled a face. 'He was all right, I guess. He
was certainly good-looking enough, but I always thought
you could do better.'

'Louise, you've floored me!'

'In that case sit down before you fall down and get
this into you,' she said drily, plopping a huge plate of
spaghetti down in front of Bonnie. 'You're looking a
bit peeky.'

Yes, well, she would, wouldn't she, after the day she'd
had? After the *week* she'd had.

'So tell me more about this man at work,' Louise went
on, sitting down in the chair opposite.

Bonnie frowned at the minute portion of food on her
sister's plate, comparing it with her own.

'Are you on a diet or something?' she quizzed, ignoring the question about Neil. 'That meal wouldn't feed
a fly.'

Louise laughed. 'Now who's sounding like a mother?
But I think I can afford to lose a few pounds, don't you?

I had to buy a size fourteen last week. I've never been a size fourteen before.'

Suddenly she looked wretched. Yet she was a very pretty woman, with thick brown hair, lovely hazel eyes and hardly a wrinkle on her face. Maybe she was no longer the size ten she had been when Stan married her but that was only to be expected.

Those lovely hazel eyes were bleak as they dropped to her plate and she started slowly twisting her fork in the spaghetti. 'Stan always said he hated fat women,' she muttered.

A quiet fury bubbled up inside Bonnie. 'For pity's sake, Louise, you're not fat! So you've put on a few pounds over the years. So what? You're forty years old. And you've had three children. You can't expect to look like you did at twenty for the rest of your life. As for Stan...well, he's hardly movie star material himself these days.'

'He's the same weight he was when we were married,' Louise argued unhappily.

'Maybe, but it's certainly distributed differently. Most of it's around his gut!'

Louise looked appalled at Bonnie's bluntness. 'For goodness' sake don't ever say that around him. He's very sensitive about his pot belly. You know, Bonnie, I think he's going through a sort of mid-life crisis. He keeps saying how bored he is with everything. I...I hope he doesn't mean he's bored with me.'

Bonnie's heart turned over but no way was she going to let her sister wallow in self-pity. Just because she'd promised she wouldn't say anything about seeing Stan with that girl, it didn't mean she was going to let her sister feel she had to take the blame for Stan's so-called mid-life crisis.

'The only person Stan is bored with, Louise,' she said firmly, 'is his own boring selfish self.'

'Stan is *not* selfish!'

'Oh, yes, he is. How long has it been since he's taken you out somewhere? Or away somewhere?'

'Well, he...he's awfully busy, Bonnie.'

'Pig's bottom! He's selfish. And he takes you for granted. Time you made him wake up to himself. Do him good if he came home tonight to find you'd gone out. Why don't you sleep over at my house?'

'Oh, but I couldn't do that!'

'Why not?'

'Because he might think things. You know...'

'Let him.'

'Bonnie, what's got into you tonight? This isn't like you.'

'Oh, yes, it is. It's very much like me. The new me, that is.'

'Then I'm not so sure I like the new you.'

'You're just not used to it. You still think of me as the stupidly romantic girl who married Keith Merrick and let him turn her into the worst kind of doormat. I won't ever be a doormat for a man again, Louise. I won't let you become a doormat either.'

'But I'm not a doormat!' she protested. 'And I'm very happy with Stan.'

'Are you? You don't look very happy tonight.'

'Nobody's happy all the time, Bonnie. Life has its ups and downs. Marriage has its ups and downs.'

'Marriage seems to have more ups and downs for the wives than the husbands, especially the wives who stay home with no money of their own, no opinion of their own and no *life* of their own!'

'Good heavens, you've become one of those feminists!'

'Too right I have.'

'And has it made you happy,' Louise argued, 'living all alone the way you do with your own money and your own opinions and your own life?'

Bonnie was taken aback for a second by Louise's counter-attack, but she wasn't going to back down. She took a couple of steadying breaths and continued, her voice calmer, even though her heart was thudding in her chest.

'Not perfectly,' she admitted. 'But I'm willing to sacrifice perfect happiness for perfect peace of mind, for being able to look at myself in the mirror and being proud of what I see. I don't wish to go into details, Louise, but being married to Keith was sheer hell. It was not what it seemed to outsiders. He was a jealous, controlling brute who abused me, both physically and emotionally. In the year before he was killed, I'd grown to fear and hate him. But I hated myself more for letting him reduce me to a quivering, cowardly wreck. I wanted to die after he died, not because I was grieving but because I didn't think I would ever be whole, or normal, again.'

'Oh, my God, Bonnie,' Louise gasped, her face draining of all colour. 'I had no idea... I didn't realise... Oh, you poor love, why didn't you tell me?'

'I was too ashamed to.'

Louise was shaking her head, clearly in shock at what she'd just heard.

'Look, I don't want to talk about it any more,' Bonnie stated firmly. 'It's over. I survived. I just wanted you to know why I am as I am.'

'No wonder you've become a man-hater.'

'I'm not a man-hater.'

'Aren't you?'

Her mind flew to Jordan. 'No. Not at all. I just don't trust them entirely. Look, let's eat our spaghetti, Louise. This is getting maudlin.'

Bonnie was aware of her sister's eyes still on her as she began to eat.

'Don't tell Stan,' she said after a couple of silent mouthfuls. 'I don't want him to know.'

She heard Louise sigh. 'I don't like keeping secrets from him, love. We tell each other everything.'

Bonnie tried not to look cynical as she glanced up. 'Maybe, but I'd prefer he didn't know this.'

'I'm not sure I wanted to know it either.' Her fork clattered as she put it down. 'Dear heaven, I... I don't think I'm very hungry any more...'

Sunday dawned muggy and overcast. The radio promised thirty degrees by lunchtime and a storm later in the day. Bonnie groaned, not being a fan of humidity. If today's weather was any guide, lord knew what summer would bring when it started next week.

Bonnie dragged herself out of bed shortly after eight, showered then pulled on a floral skirt and matching shirt which was the coolest and most comfortable outfit she owned. The skirt fell in loose folds to just above her ankles. The shirt, which she always wore out, reached down to mid-thigh. The colours—mostly reds and golds and yellows—suited her skin tones and hair colour.

Not that she cared much about her appearance that morning. Depression had taken hold by the time she'd left Louise's last night. Maybe it was the result of having talked about old ghosts. Or maybe because she'd been trying to ignore new ones. Whatever, she'd fallen into bed shortly after midnight feeling very down. She'd woken feeling no better.

Louise's words came back to haunt her as she brushed her hair.

'And has it made you happy, living all alone...?'

It had, she thought, till Jordan Vine-Hall walked into her life...

Sighing, she put down the brush then bunched her mass of curls at the nape of her neck with one hand while she secured it with a large orange clip. That done, she simply stood there for a few moments, staring at herself in the vanity mirror. What she saw was a young, attractive woman who had a lot of years ahead of her before she became a dried-up, hormone-deficient old lady who wouldn't care if she never made love again.

'Maybe you should find yourself a man,' she told her reflection. 'Not a husband. Just a man. A lover.'

It was a logical solution, but her mind's eye refused to countenance any man in her bed but Jordan. She wanted no other man, no other lover.

Tears pricked at her eyes, for she knew she could never have him. Never. He was gone. Irrevocably. Irretrievably. He wouldn't be in touch. He would not be back.

Even if by some remote possibility he did get in touch again, he didn't want her anyway. He was happily engaged. And he obviously aimed to stay that way.

She breathed in then out, a deep, shuddering sigh of acceptance and defeat. Her shoulders slumped for a moment before she straightened them again, a determined expression on her face as she lifted her chin.

Time to put her make-up on. Time to get on with living.

'You're looking a lot better,' was the first thing Gary said to her when she walked into the office.

'Thanks. So what are you doing here on a Sunday?'

'Joan's taken the kids to her mother's for the day.'

'Ahh.' Gary's penchant for vicious mother-in-law jokes had a strong basis in reality. 'Neil not in either?'

'He's out with a client.'

'Good. I hope he stays out.'

The phone started to ring then and Gary went to answer it. Daphne didn't work on a Sunday and Edgar was too mean to bring in a casual receptionist. Whoever was working that weekend and in the office answered the damned thing, and when they all went out they clicked on an answering machine.

Gary hung up five minutes later with a big grin on his face. 'Sounds like a live one. Who knows? I might give you and Neil a run for your money this quarter. Do you realise I made two sales last week?'

'That's great, Gary. And believe me, no one would be more pleased than me if you get the pewter mug next time. I've become allergic to pewter.'

Gary laughed and Bonnie smiled. But the smile was wiped from her face when Jordan suddenly walked in, looking most unJordanlike in faded blue jeans and a white T-shirt.

'Oh, God,' she couldn't help muttering under her breath, her heart immediately slamming against her ribs, colour collecting in her cheeks.

Gary, who was close enough to hear, stared with predictable surprise at her obvious fluster. His eyebrows shot up, throwing both of them such questioning glances that Bonnie felt compelled to say something to deflect his rapidly escalating curiosity.

'Good morning, Mr Vine-Hall,' she greeted him in a passably cool voice. 'I didn't expect to see you again so soon.'

Those black eyes glittered, then narrowed. 'Oh? I did say I'd be in touch...Mrs Merrick.'

Bonnie could feel her throat getting drier by the moment. 'You mean you're still interested in buying a weekender up here?'

'I mean I'm interested in buying the old house on the cliff.'

Bonnie only just managed to stifle an astonished gasp before Jordan added darkly, 'If the price is right.'

'The owner is asking three hundred thousand,' she told him shakily. 'But that's negotiable. You might get it for two-fifty, if you have cash.'

'Hey,' Gary interrupted, 'are you two talking about the McClelland place?'

'Are we?' Jordan drawled.

She nodded, her head whirling. Maybe this was all exactly what it seemed on the surface, Jordan coming back to buy a house. But she didn't think so. That electric something was back in his eyes every time they washed over her, which was continuously.

Female intuition jumped to a conclusion which took her breath away.

He wanted her. He'd come back today not just for the house, but to take what he thought she'd offered him yesterday afternoon.

Oh, God . . .

She wanted to cry, to scream, to rant and rave at fate for reawakening her sexuality with the one man she could never surrender to.

For, as much as Bonnie desired Jordan in return, she would never become involved with someone who belonged to someone else. Never! That would make her no better than Stan, who she thought was the lowest of the low, with no morals or loyalty or honour. Illicit affairs were not her style, no matter how hard her heart pounded when Jordan set those incredible black eyes on her, no matter how much she longed to be in his arms.

Bonnie almost choked when Gary slapped an arm round her shoulders. 'I've got to hand it to you, love, you're one hell of a salesgirl. Not that that place isn't a real little gem at the price,' he directed at Jordan. 'The land alone is worth the asking price. Of course, it's a pity it can't be subdivided, or the old house ever pulled down, but since it's a simple weekender you're looking for you wouldn't want to do that anyway.'

Bonnie swallowed and waited to hear what Jordan would say to that little gem of information.

'You couldn't be more right,' he returned smoothly. 'My priority is privacy, and you couldn't get a more private place than that particular house. Shall we go, Mrs Merrick? I'd like to have one last look before I decide how much I'm prepared to pay. I didn't really have enough time yesterday to see all that was on offer...'

Bonnie froze. Gary, however, raced around behind the reception desk, found the appropriate keys and tossed them over to her. 'Don't just stand there, girl. Shake a leg.' He grinned over at Jordan. 'She's a bit slow on the uptake lately. Had a virus a week or two back and we've had to crack the whip to get her going again.'

'I... I'll just get my bag,' she said, and forced her legs to move.

Bonnie stayed at her desk for a few extra seconds, while Jordan chatted away quite normally to Gary. Doubts crowded in as she watched them both together. Maybe she was wrong. Maybe her imagination had become overly heated with her own desires, projecting them on to Jordan. Maybe all he wanted was to buy that rotten old house, not...

She sucked in a sharp breath. Dear God, she'd totally forgotten about her earlier vows never to return to that place. To once again risk being manipulated by that devious old woman would be a dangerous thing to do.

Bonnie stared over at Jordan, another thought striking. Could it be that *he'd* been drawn back today because of some dastardly spell that had been put on him yesterday afternoon? Did he even *remember* what had happened between them in the library?

She didn't know. She didn't know anything, really. It was all guesswork. The only way she would find out the truth was to go with him and see for herself. It was a risk, but a risk she simply had to take. Not knowing what was behind his return visit would be too difficult to live with.

Jordan turned to look at her again as she approached, his intense gaze making her skin prickle and her senses leap. Her skirt swished around her bare legs as she walked, making her uncomfortably aware of her woman's body underneath, her only underwear below the waist a pair of white satin knickers.

'Ready?' he said.

'Yes. Where's your car?'

'Parked just across the road. I'll drive you this time, if you like.'

Bonnie hesitated, then said, 'Er ... I'd rather take my own car, if you don't mind.' The thought of being imprisoned with him in his car did things to her that were disarming to say the least.

'As you wish,' Jordan shrugged. 'You slow down as you drive past, then and I'll follow, as before.'

'All right.'

'See you later, folks.' Gary waved, turning to answer the telephone when it rang again.

Bonnie's nerves had reached screaming-point by the time she pulled up in front of the iron gates. When Jordan jumped out of his car and joined her, she just had to say something.

'To be honest, I didn't expect to see you again,' she blurted out as she fumbled with the padlock key.

Jordan laughed. 'Come now, Bonnie, that's not true and you know it. You knew I'd be back.'

Bonnie's trembling fingers stilled as her chest tightened. So now she knew the answer to one of her questions. This was not a totally innocent visit. Jordan *had* got the wrong idea about her yesterday afternoon and had come back to exploit the incident in the library.

Her dismay was deep, as was her disappointment in him. She hadn't thought he was that type of man. As much as she tried to find excuses for his behaviour she could not. The house's influence did not extend outside its walls. Jordan's decision to come back and pursue an affair with her had been made overnight without undue supernatural pressure. It was a decision based on raw, naked lust. Nothing more. Nothing less.

Bonnie shivered, her eyes lifting to find that he was looking at her with an intensity that was quite frightening.

'You're not going to buy the house, are you?' she accused, trying to sound reproachful yet ending up sounding almost desperate.

'Of course I am. It will suit my purposes very well.'

Bonnie stared across at him. 'And what *are* your purposes?'

His eyes hardened. 'Exactly what I told you the other day.'

'You...you said you wanted somewhere private where you could write in peace and quiet.'

'Correct.'

'That's it? That's *all*?'

'Should there be something else on my agenda?' he drawled.

Bonnie felt totally bewildered, till she recalled her idea that he might not even remember what had happened in the library.

'I... I suppose not,' she agreed shakily. Dear lord, she couldn't start talking about ghosts and things. He would think she was crazy!

'You've gone very quiet,' he said after a few seconds' awkward silence. 'You're not feeling sick again, are you?'

'No.'

'Good. Still, you'd better give me that key. You seem to be having trouble.' He took the old key from her frozen fingers and jammed it into the rusty lock, having a little trouble himself unlocking it. 'The first thing I'm going to put in,' he grumbled when he finally unhooked the padlock, 'is remote-controlled gates.'

Bonnie stood there quite numbly while he pushed open the gates, well aware that she was watching every movement of his surprisingly muscular body with far too hungry eyes, but unable to stop herself. If there was a case of raw, naked lust around here, it was firmly within her own weak self. She wanted Jordan as she had never wanted a man before.

He caught her staring at him when he turned to walk back towards her, forcing her to say something by way of excuse.

'You... you look different in jeans. Younger, and more... relaxed.'

He slanted her a wry look. 'Really? How odd. I'm not at all relaxed today. I must be a damned good actor. Look, let's drive on inside, shall we? This is rather ridiculous, standing out here making idle chit-chat, don't you think?'

Bonnie momentarily stared after him as he strode back to his car, before turning and doing as she was told on automatic pilot, her head and thoughts whirling. Once

again, Jordan had confused her with his cryptic remarks
and highly contradictory behaviour. She was no surer of
the real situation here than she ever was. Yet she wanted
to be, *had* to be before she went into that house.

'Why aren't you?' she asked as soon as they had both
alighted from their cars and were standing at the base
of the stone steps.

'Why aren't I what?'

'Relaxed. Why aren't you relaxed?'

'You really can't guess?' There was a hint of scorn in
his tone. 'I broke off with Erica last night.'

Bonnie's eyes flung wide. This was the last thing she'd
been expecting. Shock suspended her heartbeat for a
second, though it quickly jolted back to a fast and highly
irregular rhythm. He wasn't engaged any more...

'But *why*?'

His eyes narrowed upon her, taking in the rapid rise
and fall of her breasts. 'Well, you might be surprised,'
he said nastily. 'It wouldn't make any difference to you
if I were engaged or not, would it? You'd go to bed with
me anyway.'

She groaned her dismay and distress. 'I knew you'd
misunderstood what happened in the library.'

'I wouldn't have thought so. I still have the imprint
of your hand branded on my thigh, and your seductively
soft "darling" whispering its wicked promises in my
head.'

'But it wasn't as it seemed,' she protested. '*Truly*!'

'How very disappointing,' he drawled, his eyes
showing that he didn't believe her for a moment. 'How
was it, then?'

Bonnie knew she was going to sound crazy but she
had to try. 'It wasn't really me in there,' she insisted
fiercely. 'I told you once before, the house is haunted.
The old lady who owned it, her... her... spirit still lives

there and it wants something. I think she's trying to...'
Her voice trailed away as a coldly cynical light gleamed
in his eyes. 'You... you don't believe me.'

'No, but I have to give you full marks for originality
and imagination. Perhaps, however, you should stop to
think that telling me the house is haunted is hardly the
way to close the deal. So no more excuses, please. No
more pretending. No more games. I do know the score
and I've come to terms with it.'

'Come to terms with what?' she asked, totally confused now.

The muscles in his jaw and neck stood out as his teeth
clamped down hard in his jaw. 'Enough! I can't stand
any more. You've driven me crazy, do you know that?
Absolutely crazy. I can't sleep, can't eat, can't work. I
also can't tolerate any more of this stupid pretence or
procrastination. We're going inside, but not to see the
library first off. I think we might head for the main
bedroom.'

He stalked up on to the veranda where he whirled and
set an uncompromising black gaze on her stunned face.
'What's your problem, Bonnie?' he demanded impatiently. 'You seem at a loss. Strange... I see it as a
very black and white decision. You either come into the
house or not. You either let me make love to you or not.
What's it to be, darling? Can't you make up your mind?
Then let me give you a helping hand. I'm going to let
myself into the house with these keys. Then I'm going
to sit on the stairs, and if at the end of five minutes you
don't join me inside I'll lock up again and drive away
back to Sydney, never to darken your doorstep again.
Comprenez-vous?'

He didn't wait for her to say a word, swiftly doing as
he'd said he would, disappearing into the house. She
stood there, not moving, hardly able to think. Her mind

was in mayhem, her body not much better. To think that she had inspired such an obsessive passion. It was unbelievable, yet at the same time almost moving. What woman wouldn't like to inspire a man to feel like that about her?

So of course she was madly tempted to go into that house. How could she not be, having wanted him herself all week, having lain awake at night thinking about what it might be like to lie naked in his arms?

But, tempted as she was, the ultimatum Jordan had just delivered smacked of a lack of respect for her, and her moral fibre. He hadn't believed her when she'd denied being provocative yesterday. In fact, he'd implied that she'd deliberately tried to seduce him, maybe to help secure a sale. It was an insulting thing to think of her. Quite insulting.

But, all that aside, his offer did have a wicked appeal, didn't it? It rather suited what she had decided this very morning. That she needed a lover. Not a relationship. Or commitment. Or marriage. Just a man in her bed occasionally.

She'd even cried this morning at the thought that she would never have Jordan as her lover; had felt almost despair to think that she would never see him again. Now he was offering himself to her on a silver platter.

Really there was no decision to be made. It was a foregone conclusion.

Just before the five minutes ticked away, she started climbing the steps, her hands and heart trembling.

CHAPTER NINE

JORDAN flinched when he heard her first footstep, then shuddered.

So she was coming...

He hung his head between his knees momentarily, shutting his eyes and willing his body and mind into some sort of calm. Dear God, what would he have done if she'd walked away?

She was moving up the steps. One...two...

He leapt to his feet when she stopped, knowing that if she turned tail and ran now he'd be after her like a shot.

To do what? his conscience blasted him. Grab her, drag her in here, *force* her even? What in hell's happened to you, man? What have you become?

'I don't know,' he whispered in a tormented voice. 'I don't know...'

He simply *had* to have her. The thought had haunted him all night, obsessed him. From the moment her fingers had made contact with his flesh yesterday afternoon, from the moment she'd smiled deep into his eyes and called him darling, he'd been totally lost.

It had been all he could manage at the time to get out of that room without grabbing her then and there. No wonder Erica had jumped to the right conclusion when he'd told her on the drive back that it was all over between them. His whole body had probably *reeked* of rampant desire.

Erica...

He might have felt more regret or remorse over her if she hadn't tried to take her highly accommodating nature just too far. Frankly he'd been irritated by her willingness to kowtow to him all day yesterday. Still, when she'd told him she suspected why he was breaking it off with her, but that she was willing to turn a blind eye to his affair with Mrs Merrick provided he was discreet, he had seen red. Hell, how could Erica overlook the man she claimed to love making love to another woman? And a supposedly married woman at that! She had recognised her mistake immediately, but by then it had been too late.

Just as it was too late now not to carry this thing through to the bitter end, no matter what.

Jordan remained perfectly still at the foot of the stairs, straining to hear her step up on to the veranda. When she did, a wave of relief flooded his body, making him sway slightly. His eyes, however, remained glued to the open doorway, watching and waiting for her to appear.

What was it about her, he wondered for the umpteenth time, that had bewitched him so? It couldn't just be her physical beauty. She was lovely...yes...but no more so than a hundred other women he had met. Erica alone was more classically beautiful.

No, it was something else, something...intangible. A vulnerability perhaps?

This thought made him almost laugh. The coolly competent Mrs Merrick, vulnerable? The clever, conniving Mrs Merrick, vulnerable? That was a joke.

She was a witch, a sorceress, a caster of spells, captivating his body with her simmering sexuality, challenging his male ego with her façade of cool reserve, appealing to his darker side by presenting herself as an innocent, just waiting to be seduced.

Yet all the while she was exactly what that young chap had implied last Monday. A slut. A tramp, willing to sell herself for a sale. She'd held back when she'd thought he would buy anyway, but as soon as it had looked as if he was slipping away she'd dangled the bait, knowing damned well he would bite.

Her surprise at seeing him this morning had been just an act. She'd known he'd be back, which was why she was dressed so differently today, in softly flowing, highly accessible clothes. He'd noted the extra make-up too, as well as the perfume, which had been markedly absent yesterday, when he'd been with Erica.

Oh, yes, she'd known he'd be back, and she'd been ready for him.

His breath caught in his throat when she abruptly appeared in the doorway, wide-eyed and pale-faced, her breasts rising and falling in the most tantalising fashion.

Being on the end of her ongoing play-acting did not sit well with his painfully aroused body. 'Do you always keep your lovers waiting, Mrs Merrick?' he said brusquely. 'Or does it turn you on to have the whip-hand?'

'Jordan, don't,' she cried.

'Don't what?' he demanded, annoyed to find that her pretend distress had actually moved him.

'Don't be like that,' she said, stepping inside but staying near the doorway, as though she still might flee from him. 'There's no need. I'm not what you think. Not at all. I'll go to bed with you whether you buy this house or not. I've been wanting you too, though I tried not to show it for various reasons too complex to explain. But the main one was that till now you were an engaged man.'

His heart began pounding with her words, his head whirling. Oh, God he wanted to believe her. He really

did. But it just didn't add up. 'Various reasons' indeed.
What garbage! Besides, she'd believed him a very engaged man when she'd slid her hand up his thigh yesterday afternoon. Had she forgotten that?

No, of course she hadn't. This was just another part
of her pretence, a way of making what she did acceptable, by spinning whatever yarn sounded good, by
making the poor sucker feel she really wanted him. Then,
after he'd signed on the dotted line, it would be, Bye
bye, sucker. Well, she might find things a little different
this time. He aimed to have his money's worth, all two
hundred and fifty thousand of it!

'Well, I'm certainly not engaged any more,' he said,
his voice silky and low. If she wanted to pretend then it
was all right by him . . . as long as he got what he wanted.

When she stayed where she was, over by the door, her
demeanour still nervous, he had to battle to contain his
rapidly escalating frustration. 'Would you like to close
the door?' he asked, his voice sounding cool and controlled when inside he was shaking with an angry passion.

She did as he asked, then stood with her back against
it, her palms flat against the wood. She was beginning
to look absolutely petrified, which angered him all the
more.

'You seem agitated, Mrs Merrick,' he said in a
viciously sardonic voice as he walked slowly over to her.
'Almost as though you've never done this type of thing
before.'

She blinked at this, her eyes huge saucers as he cupped
her face. Jordan heard her suck in a sharp, almost
frightened breath when his mouth started to descend.

He hesitated, despising himself for wondering if she
might really be nervous. Women like her didn't get
nervous when a man kissed them. They opened their
mouths, and then their legs.

The thought of her doing just that for any other man but him blasted a white-hot fury through his brain. His fingers tightened around her face and his mouth swooped.

But he didn't kiss her as savagely as he intended. The feel of her lips, tentative and quivering beneath his, threw him momentarily, making him harness the urge to be violent with her, to throw her down on this floor where they stood and take her like the whore she was.

Instead, the most amazingly tender feelings rippled through his insides, squeezing at his heart and evoking a tenderness he would have thought himself incapable of at that moment. He found that he was sipping at her lips instead of crushing them, caressing them with his tongue-tip in softly soothing strokes, nibbling gently at her bottom lip till her mouth flowered apart and he could taste fully of the sweetness inside.

Stars exploded in his head when she moaned under the first foray of his tongue. He felt her melt against him, felt her own tongue dance in desperation against his, felt her utter surrender to whatever he wanted to do, to her mouth, her body, her very being. He'd never sensed such an abandoned submission in a woman before and it quite blew him away.

Maybe this was part of her act. Maybe she was used to doing whatever was necessary to get what she ultimately wanted. Money. Sales. Success.

He didn't know and at that moment he didn't care. The knowledge that she was his to command sent a dizzying sense of power through him, and his barely controlled passion burst into savage life.

Wrenching his mouth away, he took her hands and lifted them high above her head, his fingers spearing between hers as he pinned her roughly to the door. Her cry of pain found no mercy in him and he pulled her up on to tiptoe till her mouth was on a level with his, the action causing her full breasts to rub with erotic voluptuousness against his chest.

Suddenly, he wanted no clothes covering her breasts, or any part of her body. He wanted her naked against that door, wanted to see what she was hiding beneath the loosely fitting clothes she seemed to favour. Maybe her bust wasn't as luscious as it seemed . . .

He began rubbing his chest against her, feeling the size and shape of her breasts through her clothes. God, but they were glorious, high and full and firm. He could even feel her nipples, growing harder and larger by the second.

'I want you naked,' he growled, and she gasped. He thought it was a gasp of protest, but when he stared into her face he was stunned by the depth of arousal he saw there, her green eyes glazed with desire, her lips remaining wantonly apart. If this was an act, he thought darkly, it was a damned good one. Even as he peered down at that mouth, her tongue made an agitated sweep of her obviously parched lips and her eyes closed on a raw whimper of need.

He needed no further encouragement, letting her arms fall limply to her side while he worked on the buttons of her blouse, stripping the garment back over her shoulders and wrenching it downwards, tossing it aside after it peeled off her hands. The sight of her magnificent breasts, inadequately encased in a white satin half-cup bra, sent hot blood roaring through his veins. The ache in his loins flared to unbearable proportions and it was with shaking hands that he jerked the straps off her shoulders and yanked downwards, her breasts springing free as the bra fell to her waist.

Jordan had never really been a breast man before, having always favoured women with neat, slender figures. But the sight of Bonnie's bare breasts, their heavy lushness crowned by the most suckable nipples he had even seen, sent hotly arousing images into his already spinning head.

He imagined her never wearing a bra from this day forward, those glorious breasts always unfettered beneath her clothing, always ready for his touch. Perhaps he would command her never to wear any underwear at all. That way she would be his for the taking, any place, any time. Hell, he would buy a hundred houses from her if only she would let him do with her as he pleased.

Somehow she was totally naked against the door and he had no idea how she'd got that way. Had she stripped off the rest of her clothes while he'd been busy with his fantasies? Or had his hands worked with a blind, feverish will even while his darkest desires had taken shape within his mind?

His fogged brain cleared to take in her quite extraordinary beauty. Dear God, how could he have ever thought to compare her with Erica, or any other woman he had known? This was what a woman should be. He especially adored the way her tiny waist contrasted with the lush curves of her bust and hips. When he reached out to span it with his hands, his extra-long fingers almost touched at the back.

He began to squeeze, wanting to close the circle of his possession. His fingertips touched and he groaned, knowing that *he* was the captive creature here, not her. The realisation tormented him, and he resolved to make her squirm beneath his hands, make her pant with desire.

He released his grip on her waist and slid his hands palm upwards to her breasts, rubbing both nipples with his thumbs till she was making little mewing sounds of pleasure. He watched, fascinated, as the dusky pink aureoles of her breasts almost doubled in size, the already

large nipples distending till it was all he could do not to
bend and suck at them. Only the sure knowledge that
she was aching for him to do just that stopped him.

He was not her sex slave.

Not yet, anyway.

He moved his hands downwards, over the soft swell
of her stomach, down to where golden curls covered the
V between her thighs. He bypassed the temptation to
kneel and bury his face within, stroking her thighs instead, his breath quickening when her legs moved far
enough apart to give him easy access to her most intimate places.

He could not resist at least touching her there, and
when he encountered decidedly damp curls his pulse-rate
went mad. Hell, he couldn't bear much more of this self-
torture. His fingers went further, and he almost lost
control. When she began to tremble he knew he couldn't
be far off coming and that was the last thing he wanted.
So he avoided touching her in her most sensitive spot,
delving instead into the hot valley of her womanhood.
Her flesh immediately gripped him hard, pulsing against
his hand with a ragged rhythm, telling him how desperate she was for release, startling him with the wan-
tonness of her passion.

Her cry of despair when he abandoned her satisfied
his need to see her in the same hell he had been in all
week. Yet still it wasn't enough. He wanted to hear her
express her need in words, wanted her to confess to what
she was—a whore who would do anything with any man,
an exquisitely beautiful, appallingly corrupt creature
whom even the most decent man would have trouble
resisting.

'Tell me what you want,' he rasped against her panting
mouth. 'Say it out loud.'

'You,' she cried. 'I want you.'

'No, not necessarily me,' he denied hoarsely. 'Any man would do, wouldn't it? Any man. Any hand. Any——'

'No!' she broke in, her voice and body shaking. 'Only you, Jordan. Only you!'

He groaned his torment. Lord, he almost believed her.

'Now,' she insisted fiercely, snaking her arms up around his neck and pressing her nakedness against him. 'Upstairs. Quickly. In the main bedroom...'

He groaned again and swept her up into his arms, his mouth crashing down on hers as he carried her swiftly up the stairs. His feet seemed to know automatically which way to go to find the bedroom she'd mentioned, turning left at the landing, kicking open the door so harshly that it almost fell off its hinges.

He frowned as he glanced around the large room, which was eerily empty except for the huge brass bed against the far wall. The sun was streaming in through the lace-curtained window and in the distance he could see the ocean, cool and blue and serene.

It was not the view which drew him, however, but the bed, and it was to the bed he walked, laying the wantonly naked creature in his arms across the cream lace quilt, then standing back to stare down at her, thinking to himself that she was better suited to leather than lace.

Those lovely green eyes flickered open to look up at him and he was lost again, torn in two by the haunting vulnerability in her gaze. One part of him wanted to beat her for her wickedness, the rest wanted to sink down into her warm woman's body and forget, forget everything but the unbridled pleasure he knew he would find there.

Annoyed by his ongoing ambivalence towards her, he reefed his T-shirt over his head, tossing it aside then snapping open his jeans, yanking down the zip. With a violent downward movement, he peeled them off, all the while drinking in her erotic beauty, despising himself for being so stupid as to keep letting her seemingly innocent face con him. Last to go were his shoes and socks, and then he was as naked as she was, more naked perhaps because she could see how aroused he was, how much he wanted her.

This too annoyed him, especially when her gaze fed openly upon him. When she reached up to free her hair from its clasp and began spreading it with seemingly unconscious sensuality over the edge of the bed, he was lost again.

He groaned under the torture of his desire, yet still held back, partly to savour her glorious body a little longer, to wallow in her beauty and her sensual abandon, but mostly to make her wait for him, make her ache as he was aching. Besides, there was something he had to do first, a precaution that had to be taken.

But when she moaned her frustration, running her hands down over her breasts, he was transfixed. Down, down those slender fingers travelled, down between her legs, her thighs parting, her knees lifting, her back arching on a voluptuous sigh. Good God, surely she wasn't going to touch herself, give herself the pleasure *he* wanted to give her?

With a tortured sob he fell upon her, thrusting her hands away and urging his titanic desire into the hot, wet sheath that eagerly awaited him. She accepted him with another voluptuous arch of her back, her legs lifting to wrap high around his waist. He groaned as he sank even deeper into her, her flesh enclosing him hard in its satin prison, a prison from which he feared he would never want to escape.

Frantic now, he began to surge, suddenly wanting to have done with her, believing that once he emptied himself of this hated hormonal hell he was suffering from he might return to normal.

She was moving with him, just as frantic, meeting each thrust with an upward thrust of her own, making little animal sounds in her throat. He was going to come. He could feel it roaring along like an express train, the light at the end of the tunnel in sight. There was a moment of exquisite hesitation, and then he was splintering apart with the most bittersweet climax he had ever known.

For she was climaxing with him, increasing the agony and the ecstasy, her spasms incredibly strong and almost painful, forcing him to arch his back away from her and cry out. He might have actually tried to withdraw, but he could not, his flesh solidly captive within her as she throbbed around him.

Slowly, the excruciatingly electric sensations changed to a flooding feeling of pure physical exhaustion. He slumped forward and buried his face in her hair on the bed, his breathing raw and ragged.

After a minute or two he tried to raise his head but could not. Her hands began softly stroking his hair and neck, her lips busy on his throat as she started whispering the most incredibly seductive words. Endearments mixed with promises. Sexual promises.

He'd never met the like of it before.

Amazingly, after a few minutes he actually felt his flesh begin to stir within her, something which he would have thought an impossibility. Soon he was hard enough to make love again but it was she who began moving first, though she appeared to remain still. It was inside that she was moving, her muscles squeezing then releasing him, squeezing and releasing. She whispered for him to stay still, to let her do it. Which she did, blissfully, beautifully, bewitchingly. The pleasure rose this time like a gentle swell, not a storm, but his climax was no less memorable, for once again they came together. No, not together. His orgasm seemed to immediately spark hers, as though her body was perfectly attuned to respond only to a man's satisfaction.

The thought that that might always be the case tantalised him. Even as he fell asleep in her arms, he began thinking that she would make a perfect mistress. Perfect ...

Bonnie woke with a start, Jordan's body still heavy upon her.

The reality of what she had done came back with a rush and she groaned, knowing that everything she had allowed and enjoyed and actively pursued could not be blamed on any supernatural possession but her own wickedly weak nature. She'd surrendered to the seductive pleasures of the flesh once more, uncaring in the end that Jordan thought badly of her, prepared to overlook this so that she could enjoy the mindless pleasure of his hands on her, and the ultimate release that she'd known she would find in his body.

But now that her senses were clear and calm, her hormones had stopped raging and her lust for Jordan was at least temporarily appeased, she was consumed with shame. Not for any of the things she had said and done— she didn't find anything shameful in sex itself—but that she had said and done such things with a man who neither liked her nor respected her. Love she neither wanted nor trusted. But she expected any lover of hers at least to think well of her.

Jordan didn't. He clearly didn't. He actually seemed to think, in much the same way Neil did, that she was in the habit of trying to seduce her clients.

Why, she agonised, did men like to jump to rotten conclusions about women? Keith had done the same, thinking she was having affairs all over the place. They were such hypocrites, maybe because they themselves had few scruples where sex was concerned. Keith, she'd found out after his death, had not been faithful to her. Stan wasn't. As for Jordan...

Bonnie's stomach churned at the sudden thought that maybe he had lied to her about having broken his engagement to Erica. Maybe he'd just said that to facilitate getting *her* into bed. It did seem odd that he would break his engagement for a woman he only lusted after.

The distinct sound of a door opening and shutting blasted this last train of thought from Bonnie's head. Immediately, the hairs on the back of her neck stood up on end, goose-bumps breaking out all over her arms. Someone—or something—was in the house with them.

Everything inside her froze.

Strange. Up till now her suspicion that the house was haunted had not really scared her. Possibly because she'd been so sure that the ghosts, though meddling, were friendly ones.

But fear was her overriding emotion now as her straining ears picked up the sound of footsteps on the stairs. Only when she heard those footsteps pass the landing and begin to approach this room did the fear become panic, the realisation flooding her that this wasn't a ghostly apparition approaching, but a real live human being who was about to see her lying naked under Jordan's equally naked body.

'Jordan,' she whispered fiercely, and desperately tried to rouse him, pushing at his shoulders and heaving her hips up and down in a vain effort to dislodge him from her body.

'What?' he mumbled thickly, his head slowly lifting, bleary black eyes blinking open.

'There's someone coming!'

He muttered an expletive and was rolling from her when Neil's cold voice cut through the stifling heat in the room.

'I should have realised why you were taking so long. Gary told me where you were—and with whom—but stupid me started worrying when you failed to return. I even imagined your car might have broken down along that deserted road.' His laugh was harshly cynical. 'I should have known better.'

CHAPTER TEN

'STILL, you really shouldn't leave these where anyone can find them,' Neil went on, dangling her white satin panties from a contemptuously held finger. 'Not that *I'm* shocked, mind. I'm already well aware how you conduct business, sweetie. But I'm not sure Edgar has twigged yet and I doubt he would be pleased if word of your daytime dalliances got back to him. He's a proud man and I'm sure he imagines he has exclusive access to his girlfriend. Discretion, darling, is always the name of the game.'

Bonnie groaned her distress. This wasn't happening to her. It was a nightmare!

Suddenly aware of Neil's lecherous eyes on her nakedness, she snatched a handful of cream lace quilt and dragged it up over her body, clutching it around her breasts. Jordan, who had swung his feet over the side of the bed at the first sound of Neil's voice, glared back over his shoulder at her, an angry red flush staining his cheekbones.

'Who the hell is Edgar?' he snapped.

'He...he...'

'He's her boss. Didn't she tell you about Edgar?' Neil's laugh was insultingly dry. 'No, I don't suppose she did. Bonnie's not renowned for her honesty, or her loyalty. She gave her husband many a headache before he died, poor chap. He used to drink himself silly, worrying about what she was doing behind his back.'

'That's a lie!' Bonnie cried out. 'Jordan, he's lying. He's getting back at me for not going out with him, that's all. He's nothing but a nasty, vindictive bastard!'

Jordan turned his back on her and started pulling on his jeans, his silence screaming to Bonnie that he didn't believe her. Not for a moment.

Neil laughed again. 'Give it up, Bonnie. The man knows what you are. He's known all along. I warned him last Monday before he ever set eyes on you but I see he chose not to take any notice. Not that I blame you, dear chap. She's a delectable piece, our Bonnie, isn't she? Lord knows how Edgar at fifty thought he could keep such a girl happy in bed but he probably fantasises that he does, so I won't tell him what she's up to on the side. Of course, I might have to get something in exchange for this favour. Maybe sweet Bonnie can work off my silence in her own inimitable way,' he jeered. 'Or maybe, if you want to keep her all to yourself, a suitable financial reward might suffice?'

Bonnie's head was whirling as the full import of Neil's vile words sank in. He'd told Jordan last *Monday* that she was amoral and promiscuous? *Before* they'd even met?

It explained so much. Jordan's initial attitude towards her that day. His swinging moods. Then his easy acceptance that the incident in the library had been a deliberate sexual come-on.

And while her outrage was directed mostly towards Neil for spreading such an appalling lie about her, she reserved a good measure for Jordan. He'd been very quick to believe it, hadn't he? Quick to take advantage, too, once he thought he could have some free and easy sex. His assertion that he'd broken his engagement was probably a lie too.

Jordan stood up, jerking up the zip of his jeans and snapping the waistband shut. 'The only thing *you'll* be getting, *dear chap*,' he ground out, 'is my fist in your filthy mouth.'

Bonnie was startled by this seeming defence of her. Maybe she was wrong. Maybe Jordan hadn't believed Neil and he was now standing up for her. Hope gripped her heart, making it race madly.

'Tut-tut,' Neil drawled. 'I don't think so, Mr Vine-Hall. An esteemed queen's counsel like yourself doesn't go round committing unprovoked assault. He might find himself disbarred. No, I think you'll pay up, if you want to keep this quiet.'

'I won't be paying a single cent to you, you revolting little creep. As for my being disbarred... I suggest you worry more about your own pathetic hide, if you know what's good for you. Blackmail is a crime, or didn't you know that? I have good connections in the police force, so I suggest you watch yourself. Not that I give a damn whom you tell about this. I have no fear of people knowing about my relationship with Bonnie.'

'Not even your fiancée?' Neil sneered.

'I have no fiancée,' he stated, and Bonnie's hopes soared.

'That's not the way I heard it.'

'Then you heard wrong. Perhaps you hear wrong about a lot of things.'

Neil laughed. 'God, now I've seen everything. Still, you're not the first sane man to lose his head over the delectable Mrs Merrick. Those big-eyed innocent looks she gives you can be damned convincing, I'll give her that. But every time you begin to think she's an innocent, just remember where I found these,' he said, twirling her panties. 'Let me assure you, our Bonnie takes them off quick for any man.'

With that he tossed the panties across the room and they hooked over one of the bedposts, hanging there like damning proof of her decadence. 'Best of luck to you, mate.' Neil laughed again as he whirled on his heels. 'You're going to need it.'

Jordan said nothing while Neil's noisy retreat echoed through the old house. After the front door had been banged shut, he shuddered then bent to pick up his T-shirt, dragging it over his head. When the sound of Neil's car died away, he turned to face where Bonnie was still huddled up in the bed, feeling totally wretched. Even Jordan's defence of her had not wiped away the shame she had felt when Neil had walked in, or the horrors she would have to face at work in future.

'When was the last time you slept with this boss of yours?' was the first question Jordan asked.

Bonnie groaned and shut her eyes, any hopes she had been harbouring dying a quick death. Jordan hadn't really believed her. He'd merely stuck up for her in front of Neil because not to do so would have made him look a gullible fool. It had been his own honour he'd been protecting, not hers.

'I asked you a question, dammit!' he bit out in a cold, hard voice. 'I want an answer and I want it now.'

Her eyes did open, but with a sudden fury flaring in them. In just such a way had Keith always cross-questioned her, with the same bullying manner and voice. Her indignation was fierce, her resolve not to put up with such treatment from another man even more so.

'Don't you take that tone with me, Jordan Vine-Hall,' she counter-attacked hotly. 'I don't have to answer to you. Who I've slept with—or when—is none of your business.'

'I think differently,' he bit out. 'So tell me, have you been sleeping with this Edgar this past week?'

'Have you slept with Erica?' she hurled back at him.

When a guilty flush slanted across his cheekbones, it brought a pain so sharp and deep that she almost burst into tears. Instead she exploded into an uncontrollable temper. 'You hypocritical bastard! How dare you judge me? How dare you?'

'I was trying to forget you, dammit.'

There was no reasoning with Bonnie now. She was blind with rage, and outrage. An insatiable need for vengeance on the whole male race sent vicious words to her lips, words which could never be taken back later, no matter how much she might want to.

'Is that so?' she spat. 'Well, maybe I was trying to forget *you* every time I visited Edgar. You must have been on my mind one hell of a lot because I had to stay back at the office every single night. Have you tried it on a desk, darling? It's not all that comfortable for the woman but men seem to like it. Frankly, I much prefer the floor but Edgar has arthritis and——'

His hand whipped up to slap her, Bonnie's gasp of horror stopping the blow in mid-flight.

'Oh, go on!' she taunted even while her whole body trembled with fear. 'Hit me! That's what men do when they can't solve their problems any other way.'

There was no mistaking the real anguish on his face— this was obviously not the sort of behaviour Jordan Vine-Hall usually indulged in—and somewhere at the back of her shocked mind Bonnie did wonder if it was something in *her* that brought out the animal in men. Still, forgiving and understanding Jordan did not suit her purpose at this point in time.

He had to go. That much was clear. His sexual power over her was too strong and she refused to walk this path again. Even if he grovelled at her feet, she wouldn't be letting him touch her again.

'Bonnie,' he groaned, 'I'm sorry, I——'

'Don't bother to apologise,' she cut in, her voice chillingly calm now. 'I expected no less.'

Clearly he was stunned, both by her words and her demeanour.

'I don't make a *habit* of hitting women!' he protested.

'Only whores,' she pointed out drily.

'Not even whores!'

Her smile was not at all nice. 'How very comforting. Pardon me if I choose not to trust that claim. Please go.'

He hesitated, his face torn, and immediately Bonnie felt her heart go out to him. Her sympathetic reaction both appalled and disturbed her. Dear heaven, she had to get him away from her out of this house. *Now!*

'Unless of course you'd like to come back to the office with me and sign for this house,' she swept on with acid sweetness. 'Edgar should be there. He'll be very pleased since he considered this place a white elephant. Oh, and by the way, Neil was wrong. Edgar knows all about my daytime dalliances. It turns him on to think of me with another man.'

Bonnie watched as all the blood drained from Jordan's face, and she felt sick to the core of her being. If this was vengeance, or self-protection, she could not stomach any more. Fortunately, she didn't have to. He gave her one last long contemptuous look, then turned and strode from the room.

Immediately she opened her mouth to scream at him to come back so that she could tell him she'd been lying, that he was the only man other than her husband that she had ever made love to and it had been much more special than it had ever been with Keith, much more unforgettable. But the knowledge that he would never really believe her kept her silent. Everything was totally ruined.

She could not—*would* not—keep sleeping with a man who thought she was a whore. She had to have more pride than that.

But the sound of each receding footstep was like a physical blow, making her moan softly in distress. By the time he left the house and drove away, Bonnie already missed him, a bleak emptiness filling her body and her heart. The future seemed intolerable...unbearably lonely and wretched in every way. She no longer wanted to work in the place she was working in, or even to live in the house she was living in. Where once she had been happy to be all by herself, she now saw nothing but misery in her loneliness.

She wanted to cry but oddly enough the tears stayed away. She found herself staring almost blankly into space for ages and ages. Eventually, she felt compelled to move, and almost robotically sat up and swung her feet over on to the floor. Wrapping the quilt around herself like a Roman toga, she stood up and shuffled across the room and through the open doorway. She wasn't exactly sure where she was going or what she was going to do—maybe it was in her mind to gather up her clothes and get dressed—but as she carefully made her way to the landing at the top of the stairs her eyes were unconsciously drawn towards another open door.

Bonnie frowned. Why was the nursery door open? Who had opened it?

The answer brought a wry little smile to Bonnie's lips. Mrs McClelland was up to her old tricks again.

Intrigued but not fearful, Bonnie ventured into the room, curious as to what experience awaited her within. She guessed something would.

The room was quite dim, thick black clouds having blanketed out the sunlight which would normally have been streaming through the window. Any eeriness was reserved for the inky sky outside, however, and Bonnie moved to sit in the now familiar spot in the window-seat and stare out at the gathering storm. A roll of thunder shook the house and Bonnie gave thanks that she was not an overly imaginative sort of girl.

After the thunder there came a stillness, both outside and inside the room. There was no wind. Everything was quiet and very muggy, yet all of a sudden a small chill tickled Bonnie's legs.

She refused to be unnerved. She recognised the sign now and knew there was nothing to fear. 'Well, old woman,' she said quite resignedly, 'what is it that you really want? Tell me, for pity's sake!'

She wasn't too surprised when there was no audible answer, but the feeling of a presence continued and gradually there came with it a soothing sense of approval which was different from Bonnie's previous experiences. Before, she'd been left feeling a type of failure, as though she had somehow let the old woman down.

'You're pleased with me, aren't you?' she said, frowning. 'Why, for heaven's sake? I've desecrated your lovely bed, used it for my own wicked gratification, and probably been treated with the contempt I deserved. I didn't love the man. I lusted after him, that's all. I'm a weak, silly girl. I've always been a weak, silly girl where sex was concerned...'

By now tears were running down her cheeks. And it was into her silent weeping that a series of sounds came, an intermittent creaking which sent Bonnie's hair up on end. Her head whipped round, and she simply stared.

It was the cradle, swinging slowly on rusty hinges.

Bonnie's eyes grew round upon it, for despite the door being open there was no breeze coming up the stairwell.

Jordan had closed the front door good and proper on his way out. Neither were there any windows open.

No... it was a sign.

Bonnie gasped as the realisation took hold.

Jordan might have gone, but he'd left a small part of himself behind. A baby was coming. A beautiful bonny baby.

Bonnie scooped in a sharp breath as she realised what it was the old lady had wanted. To have a child live in the room she had prepared all those years ago.

'All right,' she whispered, raw waves of emotion filling her heart to overflowing. 'I'll do it. I'll buy your house and I'll live in it with my baby. I give you my word, old woman. Come hell or high water, your wish will come true.'

CHAPTER ELEVEN

'WHAT on earth have you given me?' Louise asked Bonnie, her pretty face frowning as she began feeling her Christmas-wrapped parcel all over. 'It's some kind of underwear, I think,' she mused.

'For Pete's sake just open it up, Louise,' Stan snapped impatiently.

'Don't be such a spoilsport,' she retorted. 'You know I like trying to guess first. It's a nightie, isn't it?'

'Nope,' Bonnie said, smiling widely.

'Oh, I can't wait! I'll just have to see what it is.' She ripped the paper off and held up the two garments with delighted gasps. 'Look, Stan, it's a swimming costume! With a matching beach-coat! Oh, Bonnie, they're gorgeous. Oh, I just love them!'

'They're to celebrate your new figure,' Bonnie told her. Louise had been riding a bicycle around the country roads every day for the last month and was looking trim, taut and terrific.

'Wow, Mum,' Peter chimed in. 'Dad won't dare leave you sitting on the sand alone in those. They're great, Aunt Bonnie. It's about time Mum got with the times.'

Stan, Bonnie could see, was eyeing his wife's new swimming gear with wariness. 'They're rather high-cut on the leg, aren't they?' he grumbled.

'Louise has great legs,' Bonnie pointed out. 'That isn't all of my present, either. Here.' And she handed over a large brown envelope.

'What is it?' Louise said, fingering the envelope all over.

'Unless you have X-ray vision,' Bonnie teased, 'this is one present where you simply won't be able to guess by feeling.'

When Louise extracted the ticket giving her a seven-day Pacific cruise over to New Zealand and back, she squealed with excitement at first, then frowned deeply at her younger sister. 'But Bonnie, this is too much. You shouldn't have. How can you afford it? Didn't you sink all your money into that big old house you bought?'

'Not at all. My dear boss negotiated that place for me for just over two hundred thousand, then I sold my own place for more! I actually made money on the exchange, plus I earned the commission on both.'

Amazingly, it had been as simple as that, Edgar having been simply marvellous to her after she'd fronted him that awful Sunday and told him just about everything that had happened with Neil and Jordan. It had taken considerable courage for her to expose herself that way, but she simply couldn't think of any other solution. She'd known she could not go on working with Neil.

For all his faults, Edgar was a fair man. He'd bristled with indignation at the way Bonnie had been treated, especially since he knew she was nothing like both men believed. He'd astounded her by sacking Neil on the spot, thereby relieving her of one worry about the immediate future, and Neil, unable to handle the situation, had quickly left town. He'd moved to Perth, she'd heard, thankfully without spreading any nasty rumours about her before he went. Edgar, it seemed, had threatened not to give him a reference if he breathed a single word about her.

Now, four weeks later, she had already moved into her new home, had had her wonderfully comforting pregnancy confirmed—though it was still a secret—and was slowly coming to terms with the fact that Jordan was gone from her life forever.

Not a day went by that she didn't feel tears prick her eyes when she thought of him. Dear heaven but she did so hate the fact that he'd left, thinking so badly of her. She should never have said that last appalling thing about Edgar liking her being with other men. If Jordan thought she was a whore now, she had no one to blame but herself. Still, it was incredibly sad that the father of her baby despised her, sad that he would never know his child.

And Jordan never *would* get to know him or her, because Jordan was never coming back. She wouldn't be going after him either, or telling him about the baby. The first course of action would bear no fruit, except perhaps more humiliation. And the second was far too risky. What if he decided he wanted the child, that she was an unfit mother? With his connections in the justice system she might find herself losing custody, or having to share her daughter or son with a hostile father.

That was not going to happen to *her* child. No way.

'But won't you be needing that money to do the renovations you have in mind?' Louise protested, dragging Bonnie back from her thoughts which were suddenly in danger of giving her a headache.

Bonnie took her sister's hands in hers, patting them. 'Stop fussing, Louise. I won't miss the money. It was hardly a fortune, you know. The travel agent gave me a good deal. Now you don't need a passport. The boat leaves on the twenty-ninth. Just go and have a good time.'

Stan, who had taken the ticket out his wife's hands and was studying it, looked up at both sisters with a scowl of disapproval on his face. 'You expect me to let my wife go away alone on that floating brothel for a week?'

'Is that what people call it?' Bonnie said with pretend surprise. 'Goodness me, I had no idea.'

'Damn it all, Louise,' Stan went on, most put out. 'You can't just go off like that. You won't even be home on New Year's Eve!'

'But neither will you be, Stan,' Louise told her husband rather coldly. 'You told me you were going away fishing with your mates that weekend.'

'Everything's worked out fine, then, hasn't it?' Bonnie directed at Stan with a polite smile but sarcastic green eyes. 'You'll hardly miss Louise at all. She deserves a bit of a spoil after all these years waiting hand and foot on you and the boys, don't you think? The boys are old enough to fend for themselves for a few days, aren't you, boys?'

They chorused that they were, wide grins on their gleeful faces.

Later, after Louise's magnificent Christmas turkey dinner had been consumed, followed by plum pudding and custard, all washed down with far too much wine, Louise retired to her bedroom to lie down, the boys scattered to destinations unknown and Bonnie took herself off on a quiet leisurely walk around the small farm. She was walking past the grazing cows towards the small creek that ran through the back of the property when she heard hurried footsteps behind her. Turning, she was startled to see Stan running after her.

'Wait up, Bonnie,' he called out.

She waited till he caught up with her, then spoke up quite firmly before he could start. 'If you're going to whinge about my giving Louise that holiday then don't bother. You're lucky it's only a holiday. If I told my sister what I knew about you, you two-timing bastard, then you wouldn't have a wife at all. Or three respectful sons, either.'

Stan went white with shock.

'I saw you with that girl, Stan.'

'Where? Where did you see me?'

'Does it matter?'

'I . . . I haven't done anything. Not really. A few kisses here and there.'

Bonnie shook her head, her face revealing total disbelief and contempt.

'OK, OK, so it was a bit more than that. Look, I lost my head for a while, but it's all over now. I promise it won't ever happen again.'

'Who are you going fishing with, Stan?'

His guilty colour told it all.

'Louise has been a fantastic wife to you. Keep doing what you're doing and you're going to lose her. The way I see it you can do one of two things: you can let her go on this holiday while you go "fishing" or you can race off to the travel agent and exchange Louise's single ticket for a first-class double cabin. There are quite a few of those still left, I'm told. It might cost you a few dollars, but divorce is a lot more expensive, Stan, both financially and emotionally.'

He glared at her. 'God, but you're a hard bitch these days.'

Her smile was wry. 'So I've been told.'

'It's no bloody wonder you haven't found yourself another bloke. You might be a looker but any man would have to have a chisel for that big chip on your shoulder, Bonnie Merrick.'

'You think so, Stan?'

'Louise would make two of you.'

'I agree with you, so why are you risking your relationship with her?'

He scowled. 'You don't know what it's like for a man sometimes. After you've been married for a good few years, and you're not getting much at home, you start to wonder what it would be like with another woman. You crave a bit of excitement. Louise wasn't being hurt by something she didn't know about. She's not that keen on sex any more anyway.'

'Maybe she's just not too keen on the sex *you've* been giving her. A woman of Louise's age is actually in her sexual prime. Oh, go fishing by all means, Stan, but remember this. Your Louise is "another woman" to every man on that boat. Have you looked at your wife lately? She's looking good, Stan. She's also been feeling lonely and neglected. I know if she were my wife I wouldn't let her go on that boat alone, not if I valued her in any way at all.'

'In that case I'll order her not to go!'

Bonnie laughed. 'Try it, Stan. Just try it.'

'I won't be bloody well blackmailed!' he blustered.

'In that case you're going to be bloody well divorced!'

Bonnie thought Stan was going to explode. But then he suddenly calmed down, his not unattractive brown eyes narrowing on her. 'You really care about her, don't you?'

Bonnie's so-called hard heart turned over. 'Don't you, Stan?' she choked out.

He thought about it for a few seconds then nodded slowly. 'I'd die if she left me...'

'Then don't force her to. She's a proud woman.'

He nodded again then smiled. 'Too proud sometimes. Just like her sister.'

Bonnie was appalled to feel tears fill her eyes.

Stan reached out a hand and curled it gently over her shoulder. 'Don't cry, love. I didn't mean the things I said. You're a grand girl underneath. I understand now why you are as you are with men sometimes. Louise told me all about it.'

'But I . . . I asked her not to tell you!'

Stan's grin was rueful. 'Louise and I tell each other everything, love. Well . . . *nearly* everything.'

Bonnie had to smile, despite her shock. 'I don't hate men,' was all she could think of to say.

'It would be a pity if you did. I think you could make some man very happy if you took it into your head to.'

'I'd prefer some man to make *me* happy next time round.'

'I can understand that. I hope you find him, love, I really do.'

Bonnie wished a vivid image of Jordan hadn't filled her mind at that moment, but it did. He might have made her happy, if only Neil hadn't poisoned his mind about her, if only she hadn't added to that poisoning with some venom of her own.

'Let's walk, shall we?' Stan suggested, patting his belly. 'I'll need to work a bit of this off if I'm going on a cruise. Can't have my gorgeous wife looking elsewhere, can I?'

The rest of Christmas Day was really good for Bonnie. Louise was thrilled with Stan's decision to go with her on the cruise, making Bonnie feel optimistic about their marriage for the first time since she'd seen Stan with that girl.

It crossed her mind a couple of times to tell her sister her secret news, but in the end she didn't, because Louise, being Louise, might start worrying about her. Maybe she would tell all after she came back from the cruise.

By the time Bonnie arrived home at ten that night, she was ready to fall straight into bed, sleep coming quickly. When Boxing Day dawned drizzly, her plans to spend the day in the garden had to be abandoned, and she lay late in bed, tossing up between going shopping or starting on the inside of the house.

She'd asked Edgar for the week off between Christmas and New Year so that she could do the myriad jobs she'd been aching to get her hands on since moving into her new home the previous week, and he'd reluctantly agreed. She'd already had a professional kitchen-renovation firm totally redo the kitchen before moving in, complete with sparkling new appliances, and a handyman was due in the new year to replace the guttering and paint the outside of the house.

But the rest she planned on attempting herself, from the painting and wallpapering inside, to making new curtains and re-covering most of the chairs, as well as finding a few new items of furniture to fill some of the bare spots, particularly in the main bedroom.

She'd brought none of the furniture in her marital home with her, quite happily selling the house fully furnished to a retiring couple who in turn had wanted to leave their own furniture in their old home back in Sydney for their daughter, who was going to live there. Bonnie had been grateful not to bring any memories of her marriage to Keith with her.

Maybe it was perverse of her, but she just loved sleeping in old Mrs McClelland's big brass bed, finding nothing but surprisingly good feelings there. It was where she had become a complete woman again after all, and where she had conceived her child. As much as Bonnie regretted what happened afterwards, she would never regret sleeping with Jordan in that bed. Never.

In the end, she decided to shop, and after a quick shower and breakfast she went hotfoot to the local shopping mall which was already buzzing with people. She was hurrying through the book section of the department store, heading for the towels and sheets, when she walked past a stand full of baby-name books.

Immediately grinding to a halt, Bonnie began smiling fatuously as she picked up a simple but delightful one with a pink and blue cover. Naturally, she could not resist its pull and took it straight over to the nearest cashier.

She might actually have started studying the names while she was waiting in the queue but right next to her stood a basket of hard-cover books, and right on the top of the pile, marked down to six dollars, was a novel by Roger Black.

Bonnie blinked her shock. Good God, how ironic! There she was, thinking about picking a name for Jordan's secret child, when she comes face to face with one of his other secrets.

Her hand shook slightly as she picked up a copy of the book which was entitled *The Trial of Norma Peacock*. It had a lurid cover with the naked corpse of a man sprawled behind the print, a large blood-stained knife in his back.

Looking inside the back flyleaf, Bonnie saw that Roger Black was described as a lawyer in his thirties living in Sydney, and that this was his first thriller.

Her smile held some irony. Erica certainly wouldn't have liked to see Jordan described so prosaically.

Not for the first time Bonnie wondered if Jordan had gone back to his fiancée. He probably had, provided she'd agreed to take him back, of course.

Bonnie's top lip curled in contempt. She rather thought a female of Erica's ilk would crawl across the room, licking his boots, if he asked her to.

A bit like you, darling, a deep inner voice inserted nastily.

Bonnie shuddered, her fingers closing tightly round the book.

No, she argued back silently and firmly in her mind. I'm not like that any more. I would never have been in the first place if I hadn't been so afraid. It can never happen to me again. 'Never!'

'What's that, ma'am?'

Bonnie stared blankly into the eyes of the cashier. 'What?'

'You were saying something.'

'Oh. I was—er—just talking to myself. Could I have these two books, please?'

I'm not in love with him, Bonnie told herself staunchly as she drove home. But he *is* the father of my baby. I have a right to know all I can about him. A duty, even.

Five hours later she put down Jordan's book with a ragged sigh. Dear God, she thought. Was this fictional lawyer, Richard Halliday, Jordan's alter ego, or a totally imaginary character?

Bonnie rather fancied he was a dangerous fantasy, a dangerous fantasy which Jordan had been tempted to bring to life. On the surface Richard Halliday and Jordan Vine-Hall were as different as chalk and cheese, but Bonnie suspected this was the man Jordan craved to be in his darker moments, the man he had briefly become that fateful Sunday morning.

To all intents and purposes, Jordan represented the establishment. Convention. To his family and friends, he aspired to the traditional achievements of money and power and status. He was solid and dependable and supposedly moral.

Richard, on the other hand, was unpredictable, carefree, even Bohemian in his lifestyle. He spurned money for money's sake, detested the hypocrisy of the

so-called upper classes, deplored snobbishness plus the
worship of position and power. If Jordan appeared to
be a pragmatic realist, his written word reeked of romantic ideas and values. His hero was an unconven-
tional sensualist, his lovemaking, she discovered
blushingly, being as uninhibited as his thinking. All he
seemed to want from his women...and there were
many...was that they match him for wildness and
passion. Love did not come into his requirements, merely
unfailingly insatiable sexual co-operation.

It was, nevertheless, in the description of his chief bed-
partner that Bonnie's eyes were irrevocably opened.

Marielle, her name was. A soft musical name. She
was fair-haired and fair-skinned and most decidedly
curvy but with an overriding virginal quality. She was
sexy but sweet, earthy yet wholesome, passionate though
occasionally shy.

Is that what he saw in me? she wondered. Possibly...

Bonnie couldn't really be sure. She was guessing, as
she'd always been guessing about Jordan. Really, she
knew so little about him. Only the basics, as she'd told
Daphne that day. To fantasise that she could be in love
with him was wrong, for she knew she wasn't, any more
than she had been in love with Keith. It was nothing but
a physical attraction, a chemistry.

Oh, but it was stronger, stronger even than what she'd
felt for Keith; had to be to get past her defences, defences which hadn't been in place when she'd met Keith
at the tender age of eighteen. She'd been a virgin at that
time, a silly, inexperienced girl whose head had been
easily turned by a handsome face. She'd fallen into
Keith's hands like a ripe peach.

Her initial lack of orgasm during sex had not bothered
her too much, and Keith not at all. Bonnie had still found

it all very exciting having a handsome policeman for her boyfriend and lover. Keith had seemed to adore her, wanting to spend every spare moment with her, making her feel beautiful and sexy and loved. He'd encouraged her to wear sexy clothes when he took her out, parading her proudly in front of his mates before driving off somewhere and making love to her in the car.

Bonnie had never been able to relax lying half naked on the back seat of his police car, especially with the police radio going all the time and him often choosing a place where cars did occasionally drive past. In hindsight, she believed he was turned on by these things, that he had always been a little sadistic, enjoying her nervousness, excited by the thought that someone might see them together.

They were married within four months of their meeting, and it was when their lovemaking moved to a bed in the privacy of a bedroom that Bonnie found herself really enjoying sex for the first time.

Keith had seemed pleased too at first, especially when she'd started actively seeking sex from him, not just submissively accepting it. He'd introduced many other, more exotic activities to their lovemaking, which had opened new horizons to her thinking about what making love could be like.

But the increase in Bonnie's level of sexual awareness, plus her willingness to participate in their increasingly erotic love-life, had also marked the beginning of her husband's jealousy and suspicion, the beginning of the end ...

A loud toot of a horn snapped Bonnie out of her thoughts. A second toot had her rising from where she'd been lying on the old sofa in the drawing-room and hurrying towards the front window, wondering who her impatient visitor could be.

The sight that met her eyes hit her like a blow to her insides, her hand automatically covering her stomach in a defensive gesture.

For the car parked outside the gates was a sleek bronze sedan . . .

CHAPTER TWELVE

JORDAN had come back.

Bonnie squashed down the insane surge of elation, warning herself that nothing had changed here. He still thought she was a whore. Given that, there was only one reason for his return. He wanted to go whoring again.

An angry heat filled her cheeks. At least, she *hoped* it was an angry heat, and not a heat of another kind.

Another important toot of the horn sent her charging out of the front door to plant furious feet apart on the edge of the veranda, her hands coming to rest on her hips.

'Shut up that stupid damned horn,' she yelled at him, 'and go away!'

His answer was to step out of the car and slam the door.

'The gates are locked,' she yelled again. 'And they're going to stay that way.

For an answer this time he merely disappeared to one side, reappearing several seconds later on top of the crumbling stone wall. There he too stood with his feet planted angrily apart, his hands on his hips.

He looked magnificent, she thought, dressed in the same black trousers and black silk shirt he'd worn the day he'd brought Erica up here. With the sky heavily overcast above him and a quickening breeze rustling the leaves of the trees around him, he also looked very menacing. He hadn't come to do her any good, that was for sure.

Bonnie shivered.

'As you can see,' he called over in loudly vibrating tones, 'your locked gates are ineffectual in keeping me out, as would be that pathetic old front door. Be sensible, Bonnie. Let me in. I don't mean you any harm.'

What was harm? she wondered cynically. Maybe he didn't intend to hurt her physically, but what of her mental and emotional state? Could he guarantee that he wouldn't tamper with that if she let him in?

'I'm not leaving till I've spoken privately with you,' he pronounced firmly.

Bonnie could have told him that he could speak to her perfectly well *through* the gates, that she didn't have to let him in to hold a private conversation, but she bit her tongue. Making a fuss might convince him she had something to hide. Which of course she did. Better to let him in, hear what he had to say, then coolly send him on his way.

Yes, that was the way to play it.

She was already stalking out towards the gates with the keys in her hand when she realised how she was dressed. After returning home from shopping this morning, she'd thrown off her conservative going-out clothes and dragged on a pair of disreputable old jeans and a baggy white shirt which she always wore knotted around her midriff. Her breasts were bare underneath because it was warm, the day still muggy despite the rain earlier.

Her step slowed markedly, for she knew what fast movement would cause. The last thing she wanted was to inflame Jordan's desire for her body again. It was already on the edge of an incendiary conflagration of its own.

Damn it, but she was far too sexually vulnerable to this man.

She glared her exasperation at him through the gates, hating his handsome face, hating those incredible black eyes and that attractively cruel mouth.

'You've got a darned hide coming back here,' she flung at him, jamming the key into the padlock and wrenching it apart. 'I never wanted to see you again. And I thought you felt the same way about me.'

'I did,' he said drily.

She stopped and stared at him. 'Then what are you doing here?'

'I'm tying up some loose ends.'

Now she frowned. 'What on earth are you talking about?'

'I'm talking about the possible consequences of my incredibly stupid and impulsive behaviour the last time I was here. Now unlock the gates, Bonnie. I'm bringing my car inside and then I'm bringing myself inside. Meanwhile, I hope to hell that look on your face doesn't mean I have cause to worry.'

Bonnie frowned her confusion then slowly did as she was bid, pulling the gates aside while Jordan drove his car up to the steps. Slowly, she followed after the car on foot, the penny dropping by the time she joined him on the front veranda.

Realisation of what he was referring to—and it *wasn't* an illegitimate child—brought an indignant outrage. 'You hypocritical, judgemental bastard!' she flung at him. 'Who the hell do you think you are?'

'A man and a fool,' he retorted. 'I presume by this new reaction that I have no cause to worry. But surely you appreciate I had to ask, had to find out if I was at risk. I should have known better, I suppose,' he muttered. '*You're* no fool.'

'Well, that's a backhanded compliment if ever I've heard one,' she said with rising scorn. 'I'm certainly not so much of a fool that I don't know exactly what you're implying. Any whore with a brain in her head always uses condoms these days, isn't that right? Which part of that should I be grateful for, Jordan? The part where you give me credit for brains, or for being a whore?'

Her eyes flashed fury at him, but her expressions of outrage were fast becoming a façade. Desire was fanning her temper, flushing her cheeks and heating her blood. She could feel it flowing through her, between her legs and in her breasts. Her arousal found some relief in words, flung at him with a savage sneer.

'You *like* me being a whore, don't you? That's why you've come back. Not because you have any loose ends to tie up but because you want to take me to bed again. Maybe not even to bed. Maybe you'd like it out here on the veranda. Or down there in the grass. Maybe you have a thousand different fantasies you want me to fulfil for you.'

His eyes narrowed on her, black and hard and cold.

'What is it you expect me to say to that?' he bit out.

Her chin lifted. 'The truth. I expect you to say the truth.'

'All right. Yes to everything.'

She actually sagged under the impact of such brutal honesty, grabbing at the veranda railing for support.

His laughter was mocking. 'Don't tell me I've shocked you.'

Bonnie struggled to gather herself, lest he recognise her weakness for what it really was. Once the initial moment of shock had passed, she'd begun going weak at the knees, wondering what it would be like to fulfil all his fantasies, with a few of her own thrown in.

'Nothing men say or do ever shocks me,' came her scathing retort.

'I might have said the same,' he agreed bitterly, 'but I well and truly shocked myself just now. I honestly did not drive up here today with lascivious intentions in the forefront of my mind. It was seeing you again—dressed like that—which forced me to admit what lay behind my excuse for coming here.'

'So it's all *my* fault, is it?'

'I'm past assigning blame in this, Bonnie. What will be will be.'

'You think I'd have anything to do with a man who was within inches of hitting me?'

'I've felt badly about that ever since,' he returned, shaking his head. 'What can I say except that I'm sorry and it will never happen again?'

'I'll say it won't, because I'm not going to have anything to do with you ever again!' Maybe if she kept on saying it she might start believing it.

He was staring at her, at the way she'd started kneading her hands nervously together, at her high colour and shallow breathing.

'I don't believe you. I think you still want me as much as I want you.'

Deny it, you fool, the voice of common sense screamed at her. *Deny it*!

She said nothing, merely kept on staring at him.

'I'd like to stay for a while,' he said.

Bonnie blinked her bewilderment. 'Stay for a while? What on earth do you mean by that? You want to sit down and have a cup of tea or something?'

'Hardly.' His smile totally unnerved her with its razor-like edge, causing a shiver to run down then up her spine.

'Look,' he went on, softly, reasonably. 'I don't have to be back in my office till the new year. They told me down at your office that you're on holiday till then too and I thought that——'

'At *my* office?' she broke in, shaken that he'd been going round asking about her. As much as she didn't like him thinking she was a whore, she didn't want him finding out the real truth about her. He might put two and two together and come up with four. Then he might put one and one together and come up with *three*! He wasn't going to be allowed to get his hands on her baby.

'What were you doing at the office?' she demanded to know, her agitation making her sound angry. 'Who did you speak to?'

'Gary. He also told me you'd bought this place yourself and had already moved in. Nice man, that.'

I'll kill Gary, Bonnie thought.

'Why are you so angry? You're not sleeping with him too, are you?'

'No,' she snapped. 'And I'm not sleeping with Edgar either!'

'Really? What happened? Didn't your daytime dalliances turn him on any more?'

Bonnie blushed with shame as she recalled what she'd thrown at Jordan that day. God, it was no wonder he thought what he did about her. Still...she didn't dare try to explain at this late stage. There was too much at stake now.

'Let's just say things have changed in my life lately. My priorities have changed.'

'Like your buying this house?'

'That's one.'

'And what else? Are you saying you've given up your daytime dalliances as well as Edgar?'

She glared at him. 'I don't think I wish to continue this discussion. What I do with my life is none of your business.'

'Do you have a lover at the moment?' he persisted.

'Don't you mean lovers?' she countered tartly.

'Whatever.'

'Why should I answer that? What's it to you, anyway?'

'I don't want to share you.'

'You haven't got me to *share*!'

'No, but I'd like to have you. I'd like to have you very much.'

Bonnie was both disarmed and flustered when he reached out and laid a surprisingly tender palm against her cheek.

'You... you have no right,' she protested, but shakily.

'I know that,' he murmured, rubbing his thumb gently down her cheek and across her bottom lip. 'Give me the right, Bonnie,' he whispered seductively. 'Tell me you want me to stay. Tell me you still want me. Tell me what you want...' By now his thumb was going back and forth across her bottom lip, making it tingle, making *her* tingle.

Her tiny moan sent danger signals to her brain and she staggered back from him. 'What I want... is for you to... to leave.'

Even to Bonnie's own ears she sounded pathetically unconvincing. Jordan must have thought so too because he said, 'I will... in the new year. I have to return to work then,' he finished ruefully.

'And that will be the end of it?' she asked, trying not to sound desperate.

'I'm hoping a week should do it.'

Bonnie's heart twisted. Well, that spelt it out for her. Jordan obviously hoped that by then his carnal desires would be well and truly sated. He was giving himself a fantasy week, indulging in the sort of strictly sexual and transitory liaison that the fictional Richard might indulge in. But once the week was over he fully intended returning to his conventional life and his conventional morals. Maybe even to his conventional fiancée.

She was tempted to ask him about Erica then decided she might not like his answer.

'You want it all your way, don't you?' she said caustically instead.

'You're pretty selfish yourself, Bonnie, when it comes to men and sex.'

She laughed. 'You could be right there.'

'Then you agree?'

She stared deep into his eyes, into those ruthlessly determined eyes, and knew, if she said no, he would set about mercilessly seducing her till he wore her down. Better that she keep the appearance of having the upper hand right from the start.

'Maybe.'

'What do you mean by maybe?' he said sharply.

'We'll take one day at a time, shall we? I reserve the right to chuck you out the moment you're stupid enough to cross the line.'

'What line is that?'

'The line I have in my head that separates acceptable behaviour from unacceptable behaviour where men are concerned.'

'Wouldn't it be fairer if you gave me a list of rules?'

'No, I'm a fly-by-my-seat kind of girl. I make up new rules as I go along.'

'So I've noticed.'

'You seem to like it.'

'I like *you*,' he growled, and pulled her into his arms. 'That I know.'

'You don't like me, Jordan,' she said, tipping back her head as he started kissing her neck. 'You like what I do to you.'

'Mmm. You could be right.' He nuzzled an earlobe, then bit it not too gently.

Bonnie's head was swirling, as were her senses. His lips were now covering her ear, breathing hot passion inside. 'Let's go upstairs,' he rasped.

When he lifted his mouth away, a deep tremor ran through her. God, but she was hopeless. Absolutely hopeless.

But not, she hoped, helpless. Having recognised her weakness for Jordan, she could at least control her relationship with him. Tipping her head slightly on one side, she looked up into Jordan's blazing black eyes with a saucy smile. 'Upstairs, Jordan?' she mocked. 'Not on the veranda this time, or in the grass?'

His reply was to drag her to him and kiss her so hungrily that she almost lost it. But before everything spun out of control she pulled away, gasping, and, taking his hand, hauled him inside.

When he pushed her up against the wall at the bottom of the stairs and went to kiss her again, she turned her face away. 'No,' she panted. 'Not like this.'

'Not like what?'

'Not madly, or mindlessly. I want you to take your time. *No*,' she insisted quickly, excited beyond belief by what she was saying, and what she was thinking. '*I* want to take *my* time. I want to make love to *you*, Jordan, not the other way around.'

His groan sounded like a groan of delight, not disgust. Bonnie's excitement soared, her mind filling with the image of him lying naked on the bed while she did as she pleased with him.

Stretching up on tiptoe, she cupped his cheeks and kissed him with an open mouth, sending her tongue forward to tease his lips till he groaned again. But as soon as his arms tightened around her her mouth lifted. 'Patience,' she teased in a huskily sexy voice. 'You're going to like it, I can assure you...'

'Are you sure you're not Satan, dressed up as a woman?' he asked her as she drew him up the stairs and into the dimly lit bedroom.

Her laughter was soft, but sounded oh, so seductive. Somewhere in her conscious mind Bonnie was aware that what she was doing might be construed as wicked. Jordan was pretending he thought so. The Richard Halliday in him, however, was going to wallow in every moment. *She* was wallowing in every moment.

Bonnie hadn't realised till this moment how intoxicating it was, being in control. There was a dizzying sense of power, producing a desire so intense that it was beyond being wasted with a quick release. It demanded that she savour Jordan's body, not for a miserable few minutes but for long, passion-filled hours.

'You could be right, darling,' she whispered as she pulled his shirt out from the waistband of his trousers. 'Because I'm going to take you to hell and back.' One by one she flicked open the buttons, starting from the bottom and working her way slowly upwards.

He groaned when she finally parted his shirt, his eyes closing as her hands started travelling over his bare chest. The feel of his rapidly beating heart confirmed that he was excited as she was. He *wanted* her to take him to hell and back, wanted her to do things to him that no woman had ever done before.

Bonnie couldn't wait to do them all.

CHAPTER THIRTEEN

I'M HOPELESS, Bonnie groaned silently as she glanced over at the sleeping form next to her.

She'd tried to keep it all sexual, and wickedly selfish. Tried to think of nothing but her own pleasure as she'd undressed and caressed him, as she'd made him lie there while she did a slow, tantalising strip-tease, seemingly revelling in his hungry eyes, all the while pretending that she could indulge herself in such a fashion and not become emotionally involved.

What a fool she was!

Oh, it wasn't love yet. At least, she hoped not.

But somehow, as her hands and lips had trailed over his tensely straining flesh, as she'd listened to his gasps of torment and groans of ecstasy, she'd begun to care about Jordan the man, not just Jordan the beautiful male body.

It was a futile caring, of course. He didn't want her to care about him. All he wanted was for her to keep doing what she had just done: take him to hell and back.

Her heart squeezed tight as she recalled his strangled questions when she'd finally stopped torturing him and moved to take him inside her.

'Are you sure we shouldn't use something? Are you absolutely sure there's no risk?' The carefree Richard Halliday in him had temporarily succumbed to the conventionally uptight Jordan.

'Absolutely sure,' she'd told him, and bent to kiss the worry-lines from his high, wide forehead. 'You are the first man I've ever had sex with without protection.'

147

Which was true. Keith had religiously used condoms, not trusting her when it came to having a baby.

'And there's no chance of your falling pregnant?'

At this question her stomach had flipped over, her smile bitterly ironic as she'd slowly taken his desire into her own. 'Absolutely none,' she'd returned truthfully, and watched the relief wash over his face.

For a split-second she'd been tempted to throw the truth at him, wanting to see his shock when she told him she was already pregnant with his child.

But the moment of weakness had passed. Thankfully. It would have been a shallow victory, one which might have eventually been turned against her. So she'd taken his hands and lifted them on to her breasts, closed her eyes and gone on with what she'd been doing.

At that point, it hadn't been long before she'd become lost in the physical again, before she'd wiped her mind clean of everything but his flesh moving within hers, of stretched nerve-endings and a madly soaring pulse-rate. Those earlier moments of tenderness towards him had receded for a while as she'd searched blindly and self-ishly for satisfaction, willing herself not to care if and when he came.

He had, of course. Quite quickly, propelling her own over-sensitised flesh into a counter-climax so intense that she'd cried out, then collapsed, gasping, across him.

Now here she was, several minutes later, lying alone and empty beside him while he slept the sleep of a con-tented child.

'Oh, Jordan,' she sighed softly, her hands already aching to touch him again, not sexually this time, but tendering, lovingly. She wanted to hold him, to feel close to him, perhaps to lean on him. Suddenly, she felt very vulnerable and very alone.

If only he would fall in love with her. If only he would ask her to marry him. If only...

Bonnie groaned and rolled out of bed, determined to get away from Jordan's undermining presence and her own stupidly romantic dreams. Next thing, she'd start wanting him to know the truth about her. As if he would believe any pathetic attempts of hers to take back all she had allowed him to believe, not to mention all she had actually said herself! It was far too late for true confessions of that sort.

Pushing her tangled curls back from her face, she swept her white shirt up from the floor, dragging it over her nakedness and making for the door. A bath was called for, and maybe some food. She was starving, not having eaten a thing since breakfast, which was several hours ago now. It had to be mid-afternoon.

At the bedroom doorway, one last glance over her shoulder assured her that Jordan was dead to the world. By the look of him, he would be asleep for hours. Good, she thought. By the time he woke up, she would have her silly feelings well under control.

After a quick visit to the loo, Bonnie started the bath running, then tripped downstairs to get herself a reviving drink. She was downing a tall glass of chilled orange juice in her recently renovated kitchen, admiring its red cedar cupboards and sparkling white bench-tops, when her eyes landed on the plastic shopping bag.

'Good grief!' she exclaimed, realising it was the one containing the baby-name book. Sweeping it up from the counter, she stuffed it up in one of the kitchen cupboards—a high one which didn't contain a thing yet, her heart pounding at what might have happened if Jordan had come across the bag and looked in it.

Which reminded her...

Heart still pounding, she dashed out into the drawing-room where the copy of *The Trial of Norma Peacock* still lay on the sofa. Almost as bad to have Jordan find *that*! He might start thinking she was obsessed enough with him to go round hunting out his books and reading them.

Bonnie might have privately fantasised about their re-lationship ending in a happily-ever-after scenario, but common sense told her exactly where it would end—at the end of this week, with Jordan driving off into the sunset, leaving her holding the baby.

If such a cold, hard reality made her feel momentarily sick inside, it was infinitely better than another scenario—that of Jordan coming back one day, taking their baby and driving off into the sunset, leaving her behind, and totally alone.

With this sobering thought in mind, Jordan's book resolutely joined the baby book in the cupboard, after which Bonnie traipsed back upstairs, wondering and worrying now if there was any other damning evidence she might have left lying around. The folic acid tablets the doctor had prescribed came to mind. They were sitting on top of the refrigerator, to be taken every morning. Bonnie didn't think a bachelor would connect them with her being pregnant, but just to be on the safe side she would hide them later.

'Oh!' she gasped as she walked back into the bathroom. For Jordan was lying back in the bathtub, unashamedly soaking his gloriously naked body.

Jordan looked round at her startled sound, his breath catching in his throat. God, but she looked incredibly sexy, standing there in nothing but a shirt, the tail-ends of which only just reached the tops of her thighs, her deliciously firm white thighs.

'I take it this wasn't for me?' he said, trying to sound cool when he was anything but. Damn it all, a week probably wasn't going to be enough to rid him of this insatiable desire.

Not that he cared any more. Why should he have to relegate her to only a week? Why shouldn't he have her as a long-term mistress? Hell, he'd pay her if he had to.

'No, it wasn't,' she told him quite curtly.

He almost smiled at her sharp tone. Had she any idea how her prickliness turned him on? He found her a constant challenge, goading his ego and his sexuality, making him want her over and over and over.

'Nothing's to stop you joining me,' he suggested, hoping he was hiding his intense need from her. He had long accepted that she liked being in control of things, liked to dictate the sexual side of her life.

So her sudden blush astounded him. How could she possibly blush at such a suggestion when not half an hour before she'd been doing the most amazingly uninhibited things to him?

'You're *blushing*!' he said before he could think better of it.

Her blush actually heightened. 'I...I haven't had a bath with a man before,' she said, sounding and looking so gorgeously innocent all of a sudden that he was quite blown away. What was it with this woman that she could keep doing this, changing from angel to devil to angel again with such ease, and with such apparent sincerity?

'Is it compulsory that I should have?' she added, her chin lifting indignantly.

'No. But it does seem strange that a woman of your—er—undoubted experience and expertise hasn't tried such a basic erotic experience.'

'I don't find water at all erotic,' she told him crisply, her blush totally gone now.

'Really?'

'Yes, really. Not only that, I don't think that dear old tub is designed for two.'

'If we use our imagination, we don't have to take up much more room than one.'

For a long moment, she stared hard at him. Jordan found himself holding his breath, not sure of what she was thinking, not sure of anything any more. He'd never met a woman so enigmatic. She kept him dangling all the time, kept him unsure of himself as a man and a lover, something he'd never been before. It was both maddening and intriguing. All his life, things had come to him easily, especially women. Now here was this creature...this tantalising, contradictory creature... making him feel oddly inadequate, and even nervous.

'I'll wash your back if you like,' she offered abruptly. 'But I'd rather have my bath alone.'

Sitting up, he picked up the soap and held it out to her. 'Be my guest...'

Bonnie's stomach churned as she took the soap and knelt down on the bathmat, keeping her eyes averted from various sections of his body, staring instead at his relatively harmless back. She'd wanted to run from the first moment she'd found him in that bath, hating the shameless heat which had filled her face, hating the way she'd been awash with desire from the second he'd asked her to join him.

Only the realisation that her fluster had puzzled him had kept her in the room, had made her decide on this ridiculous compromise instead of actually getting in the bath with him. If he hadn't taken her by surprise, she might have handled the situation better. As it was, she'd made a right mess of it, making her even more determined to keep her head as she washed him.

'Have you brought any clothes with you?' she asked, soaping up her hands first before placing them down on his wet back and working in wide circles with the cool indifference of a professional masseuse.

'No, I haven't,' he replied. 'Like I told you, I didn't plan this. It just happened.'

'Mmm. We'll have to take you shopping, then. You can't wear the same clothes for a week and I'm not having you walking around starkers all the time.'

'Spoilsport.'

'And you'll have to help me around the house.'

'Doing what?'

'All the jobs I had lined up for this week. I plan on tackling the front garden first, then I'm going to strip off some of the old wallpaper.'

'I could be good at that,' he drawled. 'I like stripping things. I'd imagine you'd be a whiz, too.'

'Very funny. Most of the windows need new curtains as well.'

'Can't say making curtains are my forte.'

'What *is* your forte? Around the house, that is. I'm not talking about your legal or writing skills.'

His glance over his shoulder was wickedly sexy. 'You haven't given me the chance to show you yet. You seem to have a penchant for being on top.'

Bonnie's heart started doing the tango but luckily her voice remained steady and wonderfully dry. 'Promises, promises. Give me the washer, will you?'

He slapped the cloth into her hand and she slapped it on to his back, removing the soap with vigorous wipes. 'All done!' she said finally, tossing it back into the bath.

'How very disappointing. I thought you'd wash me all over.'

'Well, really,' she huffed. 'I'm not a geisha girl, you know!'

He turned to face her, a smouldering desire lurking within his half-closed eyes. 'What a shame. Would you do it if I asked nicely?'

'I...I...'

'Kiss me,' he whispered, snaking his right hand around her neck and pulling her mouth towards his.

She didn't. But she let him kiss her.

'Touch me,' he ordered next.

She didn't. But she let him take her hand and move it down into the warm water and over his distended flesh.

Her breathing by this time was as fast and shallow as his, her will-power reduced to nothing. She knelt there next to the bath, breathlessly waiting for his next move, watching wide-eyed when he picked up the dripping flannel and began wiping it down over her shirt-front, watching dry-mouthed as the cotton became thoroughly soaked and lay plastered against her breasts, her nipples poking hard against their wet prison. As if this weren't enough, he then took the soap and started rubbing it over the already aching tips.

'Oh, God,' she moaned.

'Get into this bath, then,' he suggested thickly.

'I...I can't. You're too big.'

'Yes, and I'm getting damned bigger by the moment.'

She had to laugh, and after a moment so did he.

They looked into each other's eyes and Bonnie felt her heart flood with the most deliciously warm feelings. She leant forward and kissed him sweetly on the lips. 'Well, we can't have that, can we?' she murmured.

He cupped her face and kissed her back, not so sweetly. 'Then get into this bloody bath.'

She did.

*   *   *

Jordan came out of the men's changing-room looking fresh and gorgeous in white shorts and T-shirt. 'What do you think?' he asked Bonnie.

'You look yummy,' she said, smiling as she realised she had used one of Daphne's pet phrases when talking about hunks.

Jordan seemed startled but pleased. '"Yummy"? What does "yummy" mean?'

'I'll show you later,' she said saucily. 'Add it to the pile.'

They'd already picked out a pair of blue shorts and matching T-shirt, plus a grey tracksuit, a pair of white trainers, one pair of brief black swimming-trunks, some equally brief white underwear and a white bathrobe. They were in the men's section of the Grace Brothers store at Erina Fair, which was as well-stocked as any city menswear store.

'Do you have enough money with you?' she asked.

'I never go anywhere without my American Express card.'

'You're a real Boy Scout, aren't you? Always prepared.'

'I was, till I met you. Then off went my head and on went a pumpkin.'

'Oh, you poor darling,' she teased, rather enjoying their light-hearted repartee. 'But what a fine-looking pumpkin you've used!' And, linking an arm with his, she reached up and gave him a playful kiss on the cheek. 'Now off you go and——'

Bonnie broke off abruptly when she glanced over her shoulder and looked straight into a very familiar face which at that moment was pale with shock.

'Oh, my God—Louise,' she muttered.

'What was that?' Jordan frowned, obviously not picking up what she'd said.

Bonnie gritted her teeth and decided to brazen it out. Forcing a smile to stiff lips, she gave her stunned sister a little wave. 'Hi, Louise. Jordan, turn round and meet my sister. Louise, this is Jordan Vine-Hall, a valued client of mine. The dear man needed to buy some casual clothes for summer and wanted a woman's opinion, didn't you, Jordan? He couldn't seem to find anyone else to ask, could you?'

'Oh—er—no, that's right,' he agreed, obviously at sea but doing his best to go along with her.

Louise was staring at Jordan as though he were Mel Gibson in the flesh. Bonnie wanted to groan her dismay at finding herself in such an awkward situation, her eyes pleading with Jordan not to give away the reality of their relationship.

'So what are you doing here, Louise?' Bonnie went on hurriedly. 'This is a bit far for you to come shopping, isn't it?'

'Stan needed some new clothes for the cruise and the range is much better here than in Wyong. He's over there, browsing,' she said, pointing in the direction of the shirt racks.

'I'll just duck back into the changing-room, Bonnie,' Jordan said. 'Nice to meet you, Louise.'

'And you,' Louise returned dazedly as he walked off, looking every inch the impressive professional man he was, even in shorts.

A silence fell between the two women as Louise turned a narrowing gaze back to her younger sister. Bonnie sighed at long last, deciding that to continue with the farcical pretence was silly, in view of her pregnancy. Louise would eventually have to know about the baby, and when she did perhaps she would understand, having seen Jordan for herself.

'OK, OK,' she began resignedly. 'So we're having an affair.'

Bonnie was taken aback when Louise looked delighted. 'But that's wonderful! Oh, Bonnie, he's gorgeous. Oh, I feel so happy for you.'

'For pity's sake, Louise,' Bonnie snapped, dismay making her sharp. 'It's just an affair. Nothing more. The man's a highly successful barrister up here on holiday. Come the new year he's going back to his life in Sydney and I'll never see him again. It's just sex, Louise, nothing more, nothing less.'

'It might be just sex for him, love, but it's not just sex for you. Take a good look at yourself when you get home, Bonnie Merrick. You're positively glowing! Don't go telling me you're not in love with that man.'

'I'm not in love with him,' she lied.

'I don't believe you.'

'What don't you believe, love?' Stan asked.

Bonnie's glare warned Louise not to say a single word. But then she remembered how she hadn't kept her last promise when it came to telling Stan things about her private and personal life. Bonnie decided to get in first and make sure Stan didn't hear a romanticised version of the truth.

'She doesn't believe her sweet little sister would sleep with a man she doesn't love,' she said bluntly. 'I think, Stan, you should explain to Louise that sex and love do not always go hand in hand.'

'Maybe not with some people,' Louise argued. 'But we Merrick girls aren't like that.'

'For which I am eternally grateful,' Stan said, giving his wife an affectionate squeeze. 'As for you, sister-in-law, don't bother trying to con us. We're your family and we know exactly what sort of girl you are. You'd be the last girl on earth to sleep around. Now, am I going to know who the lucky fellow is who's finally captured that elusive heart of yours?'

'He's just coming out of the changing-rooms,' Louise whispered. 'The man in black.'

Stan looked, then turned back to face Bonnie, a slightly worried frown on his face. 'I'd feel a lot better if he were wearing white.'

'And I feel a lot better when he isn't wearing anything,' Bonnie drawled.

Both of them simply stared at her, mouths gaping.

Bonnie kept a bold bland face. 'I see I've finally got my message across. Good. Now go and have a fantastic holiday, you two, and don't do anything I wouldn't do. That should give you plenty of leeway,' she added drily.

She left them, still gaping, and walked over to where Jordan was just finishing paying for his pile of purchases, the memory of their shocked faces going a long way to lessening any distress that their simplistic view of her had evoked. Jordan hooked an arm through hers, then began guiding her through the throng of shoppers towards the nearest exit, a determined expression on his face.

'Are we in a hurry or something?' she asked.

'In a way. I think you and I had better have a little talk which is long overdue.'

'What about?'

'About lots of things.'

'Name one.'

'Mrs Bonnie Merrick.'

Bonnie's stomach flipped over. 'What about her?'

'That's what I want to know. About *her*.'

'What a boring topic. I'd much rather talk about Mr Jordan Vine-Hall.'

'In that case, we'll have a fair exchange of information. We'll play twenty questions, shall we? Twenty for you and twenty for me.'

'What if you ask a question I don't want to answer?'

'Then you can pass. But you can only pass on five questions. Fair enough?'

'I might lie.'

'So might I.'

'Then what's the point?'

He smiled. 'I'll know if you lie.'

She ground to a halt. 'How? How will you know if I lie?'

'Because I'm skilled at recognising lies. It's my job.'

'I don't think that's fair. I think we should swear to tell the truth, or pass.'

'All right. Do you have a bible handy?'

'Very funny.'

'I'm not being funny.'

'In that case there's one in the library at home. I saw it there the other day when I was dusting.'

'Good. We'll make our vow of truth on that when we get home and then the questions can begin.'

'What if I want to eat first? I'm hungry.'

His sidewards glance made her heart flutter wildly. 'I'm hungry too, come to think of it. All right, we'll eat each other first then ask the questions.'

'But that's not . . . I didn't mean . . . I . . .'

'Close your mouth, woman. You don't want to catch flies, do you?'

CHAPTER FOURTEEN

'SATISFIED?' Bonnie said wryly. 'Are you sure you wouldn't prefer to sit me over at the desk and shine a bright light in my face? That is the way the SS conducted their interrogations, you know. Of course, they didn't rely on a mere oath on the bible for their answers. They kept the thumbscrews handy.'

Jordan said nothing. They were sitting facing each other, but Bonnie's chair was smaller and more upright than Jordan's overstuffed variety. He looked infinitely more relaxed than she did, though perhaps that was due to his being dressed in his new white bathrobe while she had clambered back into jeans and a shirt before coming back downstairs.

It perturbed Bonnie that the more they made love, the more uptight she became afterwards. The balance of power in the bedroom was shifting. She knew it and he knew it. And, much as she had enjoyed Jordan's masterful display over the past hour or so, it had left her feeling quite unnerved.

This time, it had been *him* taking *her* to hell and back. She'd begged him in the end to release her from her misery. But he hadn't for ages, using his greater physical strength to dominate and control her movements, or lack of them. And while it had all been incredibly arousing and exciting it had also been frightening in a way, especially when she'd found herself in a mindless void where she would have allowed him to do anything he wanted.

She'd never felt quite like that before, and it worried the life out of her. Keith had forced her to do what he wanted through fear. Jordan was beginning to achieve that end through the power of her passion for him. She wouldn't mind entrusting her body to him in that way if he really truly loved her and cared for her. But he didn't. It bothered Bonnie that he might start forcing her to do more and more kinky things during those moments when she was totally carried away.

She shuddered at the thought.

'Are you all right, Bonnie?' Jordan asked.

The warm concern in his voice relaxed her somewhat. Jordan might not be in love with her but he did care, in a weird kind of fashion. Why else would he be doing this, making her sit here while he asked her questions about herself?

Or was it just his QC curiosity, his hating having questions unanswered in his mind? Richard Halliday was like a dog with a bone when he wanted to find out some secret or other. His creator was probably of a similar ilk.

'Why don't you answer me,' Jordan suddenly ground out, 'instead of sitting there with that damned Mona Lisa smile on your face? God, but you can be an irritating woman sometimes!'

Startled by his outburst, Bonnie was nevertheless not about to be too apologetic. She'd done with being a mouse when a man decided to roar. 'Sorry,' she said nonchalantly. 'I was away in another world.'

'Oh, great! Glad to see you're really keen to do this. I would have thought you might like to find out a little about the man you're sleeping with. Or do you keep all your lovers at a nice safe distance, ready to be turfed out the moment they cross one of your invisible lines?'

'Is that question one, Jordan?' she asked coolly.

'No, it damn well isn't!'

'Good, then I don't have to answer it.'

'You bitch.'

'Speak to me that way again, *lover*,' she ground out through clenched teeth, 'and you will be turfed out, whether the week's up or not.'

They glared at each other for several moments, Jordan being the first to relinquish. 'You're right. I'm sorry. That was totally uncalled for, and most ungentlemanly of me.'

She almost choked on the spot. *Ungentlemanly*? She'd never heard a modern man use that word. There again, Jordan, in many ways, was not a modern man. He was what some people might have called a stuffed shirt. If she hadn't read that book and seen into his darker side, Bonnie would have been totally bewildered by the contradictions in his personality.

'I think, perhaps, we'd best begin,' she said crisply. 'Who goes first?'

'You, I think.'

'Why? Because you always like to have the last word?'

'Yes. That was question one, was it?' he taunted in much the same way she'd just done.

So much, Bonnie thought caustically, for his humble apology earlier.

Their eyes clashed, blazing black against glittering green.

His smile, when it came, carried enough self-mockery to be both appealing and disarming. Bonnie allowed herself a small returning smile.

'You like to live dangerously, Jordan,' she said.

He said nothing, merely continued to study her as though trying to read her mind. She smiled into his searching gaze, realising he didn't puzzle her half as much as she puzzled him. That book had revealed a good deal about its writer. Still, there were a few questions she wanted answered.

'Question one,' she began when he didn't. 'What is your relationship like with your parents and siblings?'

There was no doubt that she'd surprised him. His head snapped back hard against the chair, his eyes blinking before he gathered himself.

'I respect and admire my father, love and loathe my mother, and have no living siblings. My older brother died when he was six, leaving me to fulfil the family tradition of the eldest son becoming a judge.'

'That's not a complete answer, Jordan. I asked what your relationship was like. A relationship is a two-way thing. What do they think of *you*?'

He shrugged. 'My father is suitably proud of me, and my mother . . . worried.'

'Why is she worried?'

'That's another question.'

'Agreed. We'll call it question two. Now answer it, please.'

'I pass.'

Bonnie's frustration was acute. She wanted to know more about his relationship with his mother. It suddenly seemed very important. Why did he love and loathe her? What had the woman done? She would have to find a way to trap him into answering. But how? She needed time to think.

'Your turn,' she said, smiling sweetly.

Any smile faded at his first question.

'Were you unfaithful to your husband?'

Bonnie suppressed a sigh. So this was going to be the way of things, was it? He wanted to know all her dirty linen. What to do? Should she pass, or answer truthfully?

The wish to wipe away some of his misconceptions about her morals was very strong, and since she'd originally denied Neil's assertion that she was an adulteress there was no reason why she shouldn't tell the truth. But she would have to be careful. Deny *everything* he believed about her and he might start wondering what had driven her to have an affair with him, as well as why a normally virtuous woman would be pre-protected against pregnancy.

'No,' she said simply. 'I was not.'

She watched for a reaction on Jordan's face but there was none.

'Were you a virgin when you married him?'

Silly question. It gave her a splendid out. 'Of course not,' she said, and saw Jordan flinch.

His reaction infuriated her. 'That's two questions each,' she snapped. 'On to question three. Will you be going back to Erica after this week is over?'

'Good God, no. How could I go back to her antiseptic brand of sex after you?'

Now Bonnie flinched.

'Will *you* be going back to Edgar?' he demanded in turn. 'No doubt he'd be turned on as hell if you told him about what we've been up to.'

A telling heat immediately flooded her cheeks. 'I doubt I'll be sharing *any* intimacies, either physical or verbal, with Edgar at any time in the future.'

'I wish I could believe you,' he muttered.

Her chin lifted. 'I thought you could always tell a lie when you heard one!'

'And so I can. That's why I know there's something wrong with what you just said.'

'I told the truth!'

'Lies can be hidden within the truth. You're lying to me, Bonnie. I can feel it.'

She jumped to her feet. 'Then there's no point in continuing this, is there?'

'Oh, do sit down, for pity's sake. I can't stand hysterical women.'

'And I can't stand hypocritical men. You say you want the truth but you don't. You wouldn't be able to handle the truth if it was before you in black and white, Jordan. Not a word of it!'

He was on his feet, his hands grabbing her by the shoulders. 'What do you mean by that?'

'Is this another of your twenty questions?'

'I'm warning you, Bonnie...'

'Don't, Jordan. Don't warn me or threaten me or bully me. I won't stand for it, do you hear me? I won't be brow-beaten any more, or cross-questioned, or subjected to some pathetic inquisition. I've no idea why I agreed to this in the first place. My life is my own—past, present and future. You asked for a week of it and I agreed to give that to you, simply because having you here, having *you* gives *me* pleasure. But come the new year I want you out of this house and out of my life. *Comprenez-vous*?' she finished, as he had done once before, she recalled.

'Maybe I won't want to stay the week,' he countered savagely. 'Have you thought of that?'

'Oh, you'll stay the week, Jordan. I have no doubts about that.'

His fury became a tortured frown. 'What *are* you? Sometimes I wonder if you're a real person with real feelings.'

'I'm very real, Jordan,' she said in a strangled voice, an unexpected lump forming in her throat. There she'd been, thinking anger would carry the day and hide her vulnerabilities. But she'd been wrong. 'Very real,' she repeated in a raw whisper, tears flooding her eyes.

His groan when he saw them was full of anguish. 'Why do you do this to me?' he cried out, and gathered her tight against him. 'You're destroying me, Bonnie. I don't know who I am any more. I don't know what I want. All I can think of is you...'

'You mean all you can think of is having sex with me,' she choked out against his chest.

'Yes... No... Oh, God, I don't know. Hell, I might even be falling in love with you...'

Her heart turned over at this reluctant declaration. It was hardly the stuff dreams were made of. She pulled back, dashing the tears away from her cheeks, her smile bitterly wry. 'I doubt that, my darling.'

'Don't keep calling me that, damn you!'

'Why not?' She pressed a perversely loving hand against his cheek, and reached up to kiss him. 'You are a darling. A poor mixed-up darling. I have a feeling, however, that come the week's end you'll be ready to go back to that life you've run away from for a little while. Unless, of course, you're planning on asking for an extension. Maybe you fancy the odd fantasy weekend in your own secret love-nest every once in a while, whenever the pressure of the real world gets too great?'

His face carried shock at her words. 'Now I know what you are. You're one of those damned psychics!'

She laughed. 'I wish I were.'

He pulled her to him. 'And would you agree?' he rasped.

'To what? Being your occasional mistress?'

'Yes.'

'We'll see, Jordan. We'll see.'

'You *are* a bitch,' he ground out, his arms tightening around her. 'But it's all right. I wouldn't have you any other way.'

Bonnie could not find any smart reply to that. She was already trembling in his embrace, worries about the future whirling in her head as he bent his mouth to hers.

How was she going to be able to stop him coming back whenever he wanted? What would happen when he noticed her changing figure, when he put two and two together and realised she was expecting his child?

She didn't know the answers, and she didn't dare ask the questions. The future would have to wait, she quickly realised, for Jordan wasn't going to. Already he was pulling her down on to the threadbare carpet and tugging at her clothes.

Bonnie was bitterly aware that she should at least give some token resistance to his increasing demands, not lie there limply while he stripped her. He couldn't expect her just to do whatever he wanted, whenever he wanted, wherever he wanted it.

She was contemplating saying something when his masterful mouth found its mark. Her first moan carried a mixture of delight, dismay and self-disgust. Her second . . . just delight.

Why fight it? she thought dazedly. And didn't.

In the next few days they settled into an almost domesticated routine. Breakfast was followed by the various household chores Bonnie assigned for them that day. Jordan, she found, preferred working outside, either weeding the garden beds or attempting to make a lawn out of chaos. He was woeful with a paintbrush, and had no patience with wallpapering. By eleven, it was always hot enough to wander down for a pre-lunch swim in their own personal piece of the Pacific.

The cove was only tiny, with not a great deal of sand and a lot of rocks, but it was marvellously private, the only track down from the cliffs being on Bonnie's property. The water was good for swimming, being relatively still, the reef of rocks between the jutting head-

lands breaking up the force of the waves long before
they made the shore.

After their swim, they would return to the house, cool
and refreshed, though Jordan was invariably aroused
from seeing Bonnie in her bikini. After making love they
would tuck into a large lunch, retiring upstairs for a siesta
till mid-afternoon. On waking, Jordan would make love
to her again before rising to tackle the rest of his allotted
chores while she got on with making new curtains.
Around six they would knock off work for the day, bathe
and dress, then go out for dinner in one of the numerous
little restaurants that dotted the Central Coast.

On the night of the thirtieth, the evening before New
Year's Eve, Bonnie made the mistake of choosing to dine
at the Beachview, a popular eating spot perched on the
side of one of the hills behind Blackrock Beach. They
had just had their main meal set before them when Edgar
came in, an attractive redhead on his arm.

Jordan, noticing Bonnie's agitation at the new ar-
rivals, gave Edgar such a hard stare that he guaranteed
their own selves being noticed, despite their being in a
dimly lit corner. Bonnie groaned when Edgar, after de-
positing his date at a table, wandered over to them, giving
Bonnie's handsome companion a more than curious inspection as he approached.

'Good evening, Bonnie,' he said by way of greeting.
'Can't say I've seen you in here before.'

'I—er—this is my first visit.'

'I can see you're enjoying your holidays,' he said,
pointedly glancing Jordan's way.

'Yes,' she said succinctly, a brittle smile on her lips.
She was damned if she was going to introduce Jordan.

'Are you going to come to my New Year's Eve party
tomorrow night?'

'I don't think so, Edgar, but thanks for the invite.'

Jordan's black eyes flashed. 'Bonnie, darling,' he cut in smoothly, 'where are your manners, leaving us poor chaps dangling without a proper introduction?' He held out his hand for Edgar to shake. 'I presume you're Edgar, Bonnie's boss? I'm Jordan Vine-Hall. No doubt you've heard of me. Bonnie told me she'd mentioned me to you.'

Bonnie sucked in a sharp breath while Edgar stiffened. 'She might have,' he said coldly. 'You were a client of hers a few weeks back, weren't you?'

'That's right.'

Edgar shot an intuitive look at Bonnie's embarrassed blush, then glared back at Jordan. He looked as if he was about to say something cutting to Jordan but he didn't, thank God.

'Well, enjoy you're meal, folks,' he said instead. 'I should be getting back to my date. See you after the holidays, Bonnie. We've sure been missing you at work.'

The scowl on Jordan's face was full of a simmering rage. 'I'll bet he misses you,' he spat at her. 'So must his desk!'

'That's enough,' she spat right back. 'I have never had sex with Edgar, either on his desk or anywhere else.'

Jordan's mouth flapped open. 'You...what?'

'You heard me, Jordan. There has never been anything of a sexual nature between Edgar and myself. I lied. You wanted to believe Neil's vile accusations, and I wanted you to leave, so I lied.'

'You lied...' He seemed to be having difficulty assimilating this startling new information. 'But...but you told Edgar *something* about us. He said as much. What?'

'The truth. That Neil told you I was easy, you believed him and acted accordingly. I only told Edgar *that* much because I could no longer work with Neil. I was going to resign but he fired Neil instead and that was that.'

'Are you saying that you've never slept with a client?'

Once again, Jordan had left himself wide open with a question. For a QC, he was making some elemental mistakes.

'No,' she bit out. 'I'm not saying that. But it has never had anything to do with selling a house.'

'Then what has it to do with?'

'Sex, of course.'

'I see ...'

'Do you, Jordan?'

'I'm trying to, dammit! But you haven't exactly made it easy, telling me lies.'

'No, I don't suppose I have. But when you're hurting you do what you can to protect yourself. Especially when you've been hurt before.'

He looked at her long and hard. 'You're talking about your husband, aren't you?'

'Yes.'

'What did he do?'

'He hurt me.'

'Yes, but how? Give me an example?'

'Only one?' She made a choking sound. 'All right. The night before he died he beat me with a belt so brutally that it took months for the welts and bruises to go away.'

The breath left his lungs in a horrified gasp.

'Is that enough of an example for you?' she went on quickly, for although she sounded calm a trembling had begun on the inside. 'Or do you want to hear more?'

'No,' he shuddered, but he went on looking at her, looking and thinking.

'I've hurt you too, haven't I?' he said at last. 'Emotionally ...'

Her eyes suddenly filled.

'God, Bonnie.'

She stood up abruptly and fled the restaurant. He found her leaning on her car, sobbing.

'Bonnie, don't,' he groaned, turning her round and taking her in his arms. 'Oh, God, darling, don't.'

'Take me home, Jordan,' she wept against his shirt-front. 'Don't question me any more. Don't make me tell you things. Just take me home and hold me.'

'All right. Let me get your things and pay the bill.'

He was as good as his word. He took her home and put her to bed, then climbed in beside her and just held her. He didn't ask her questions or try to get her to talk. He didn't even make love to her. She cried on and off then eventually fell asleep in his arms.

She woke to silence, a rapidly heating room and a note attached to Jordan's pillow.

'You've slept in,' it said. 'If you can't hear the Whipper Snipper, I've gone for a swim.'

Bonnie rolled over and a bead of perspiration ran down between her breasts. She slid a hand under her hair and felt its dampness. A swim was definitely in order but she was reluctant to face Jordan after last night. What must he think of her?

Perhaps if she just acted as though nothing had happened, if she kept refusing to talk about the past, in the same way as she was trying not to think about the future, she would be able to cope without cracking up till after he left in the new year. That was only a couple of days away.

Dragging on her bikini, she draped a towel around her shoulders and set off for the cove.

Jordan shouted and waved from the water once he spotted her on the cliff trail, Bonnie squinting down at him in the bright sunshine, her heart fluttering as she realised he was skinny-dipping. He always wore his costume when she was with him, but this time, obviously thinking he would be alone, he hadn't bothered.

It was silly to feel embarrassed, after all they had shared, but there was something about outdoor nudity that unnerved Bonnie. Though totally uninhibited in private, she was not a person to enjoy lovemaking anywhere even remotely public.

'Come on!' Jordan shouted. 'It's terrific in.'

Determined to ignore his nakedness, she hurried on down the path, tossing the towel away and running into the water, grinding to a halt when the chill of the water took her breath away.

'It's freezing!' she cried, hands flapping wildly.

'You'll soon get used to it,' he said, surging through the water towards her.

Immediately she panicked. 'No, don't! Don't come near me.'

'I won't splash you. I promise.'

He stood up in front of her, water cascading from his elbows when he lifted his hands to slick back his hair from his face. Water was streaming off other parts of him and she couldn't help staring, or wanting.

Her staring unfortunately brought about a dramatic change in his body. Bonnie blushed while Jordan merely laughed.

'What a fortune I would make if I could bottle what you do to me,' he growled, and went to draw her into his arms.

'Don't touch me!' Bonnie exclaimed, struggling backwards and almost falling back into the water.

Jordan was clearly taken aback. 'Why not?' he asked, frowning. 'What's wrong?'

'Nothing's wrong,' she explained breathlessly. 'I...I just don't want to do anything *here*.'

He glanced around, startled. 'But why on earth not? We couldn't be any more alone if we were in a bedroom.'

'Perhaps, but I...I'm shy.'

'Don't give me that, Bonnie. You haven't a shy bone in your body when it comes to making love. You're just punishing me, aren't you? For believing Neil. For believing all the things I believed about you.'

'No!' she gasped.

'Then let me make love to you. Here. Now. Or are you going to trot out that old excuse about you not finding water erotic? Look, stop being silly, darling. I love the woman that you are. I love *you*, and I want to make love to you.'

Bonnie was dazed by this highly unexpected declaration of love. 'You love me?' she asked, her voice and heart cracking.

His smile was both tender and wry. 'Love you? I adore you, don't you know that?'

'No.'

'Darling Bonnie, I'm crazy about you. And I simply can't get enough of you.' He started caressing her shoulders, and then her breasts, teasing the nipples to hardness before turning her round and undoing the bratop, letting it drop into the sea. She stood, oddly frozen, as he peeled the panties down her legs, robotic in her lifting of each foot so that they too could float away on the gently lapping waters, leaving her naked and defenceless against his desire.

'You're so beautiful,' he whispered, his head dipping over her neck to kiss her throat while he continued to play with her breasts. 'You're the most beautiful, sexiest woman in the world...'

Even while Bonnie was finding pleasure in his words and hands, her eyes nervously scanned the heavily scrubbed cliffs. Anybody could be hiding there, she began to worry. Jordan's hands moved down over the flat plane of her stomach, over her hips and buttocks. His caresses became very intimate, making her breath quicken and her senses spin. Waves of pleasure started to lap through her, and she moaned softly. Her body kept telling her to surrender, just to let him do it then and there.

But her head was still rebelling.

'No,' she moaned.

It hardly sounded like a protest, but to give him credit Jordan hesitated. 'What do you mean, no?' he said. 'You can't expect me to stop. God, Bonnie, I love you. I need you.'

A memory crashed into her mind, of Keith forcing himself on her that last night, all the while telling her how much he loved and needed her.

'No,' she croaked, the memory having brought with it a very real nausea.

His arms went around her waist, tight and threatening. She could feel his arousal against her buttocks, feel its throbbing life and aggressive need. Her head began to whirl. He wasn't going to stop. He was going to go ahead and just do it, whether she wanted him to or not.

Panic-stricken, she broke free of his hold and started to run, but the water dragged at her legs and there were far too many holes in the soft sand. Crashing down on to her hands and knees in the shallows, she almost died when she felt his body loom over hers from behind.

'Oh, God, no,' she whimpered.

For a few mad moments she fought him, till she finally realised he was only trying to pick her up out of the water. Bonnie sagged with the rush of relief, her suddenly limp body falling down through his slippery hold back into a huddle in the shallows.

'No, don't,' she sobbed when he went to pick her up again. 'Leave me...'

'I can't do that, Bonnie. Let me help you.'

'No!' she screamed. 'You can't help me. No one can help me. Go away, I tell you. You don't love me. Not the way I need to be loved. No man will ever love me that way. Go away, Jordan. Just go away.'

She buried her face in her hands and wept, wept till there were no tears left. When she finally lifted her ravaged face, the cove was deserted. When she staggered back to the house, it too was deserted.

It took her several minutes to come to terms with what she had done. She'd told Jordan to go...

And he had.

CHAPTER FIFTEEN

GONE.

Bonnie wandered through each room of the empty house a second time, searching for some sign that Jordan hadn't really gone, that he would be back later. She ended up in the main bedroom, a momentary hope flaring when she discovered he'd left behind the clothes they had bought together. Till she realised he wouldn't have wanted to take them back to his real life. They had been part of the fantasy. And the fantasy was now over, just as their love-affair was over.

A sob was torn from her throat as she buried her face in her hands. The affair part might be over but the love would live on forever. Louise had been so right about that. She did love Jordan, so much so that to contemplate life without him was unbearable. How would she ever make it through each day? And each night?

Bonnie sank down on to the side of the bed where they'd spent so many incredible hours, tears streaming down her face as she tipped sideways on to the pillows. Her hand reached out to stroke the side where Jordan had slept and her heart ached with missing him already.

Yet she'd been right in what she'd said to him, hadn't she? He didn't love her as she needed to be loved. Otherwise he wouldn't have left her like this. He would have stayed, no matter what she said.

His love—such as it was—had been a physical thing. There'd been no real future in it. Not the sort of future she needed after her experience with Keith.

She needed the man in her life to prove to her that she had his total love and trust—not just lust—and that she came first in his life, now and forever.

Let's face it, Bonnie, she told herself wearily. Jordan was never going to marry you. The only role in his life you were going to be offered was mistress, not wife, lover, not beloved.

Still . . . at the moment, she would settle for anything if it meant he would come back.

'Oh, Jordan,' she cried, and clasped his pillow to her, hugging it fiercely. 'Come back, my darling. Please come back!'

But he didn't come back.

The hours ticked away. The sun set and the moon came out, its soft light trickling through the lace curtains. Finally, Bonnie released Jordan's pillow and rolled from the bed to carry herself on leaden legs over to the window. Pushing back the lace, she was staring out at the darkened ocean when she saw something glinting out of the corner of her eye.

It was coming from a far corner of the still ramshackle back garden, where the trees and bushes were very thick. Was it a piece of metal shining in the moonlight? she wondered. An old iron seat perhaps, under the trees?

The urge to go and see for herself was incredibly strong, so strong that it seemed out of all proportion to the situation. Who cared what it was?

Suddenly, everything inside Bonnie froze. It was the old lady again, she accepted with a little shiver, directing things from beyond. What did she want this time? What could possibly be out in that garden that was of any relevance?

Within seconds, Bonnie found herself being propelled down the stairs and out of the back door. Amazingly,

she found a small path she'd never noticed before which
led her past some overgrown shrubs and under a leafy
elm into a relatively cleared grass circle, in the middle
of which were two graves with matching headstones.

A shaft of moonlight was glancing off the one on the
left which read:

Here lies Matthew McClelland, May 1918—July 1946,
beloved husband of Dulcie McClelland. War destroyed his body but never his spirit or his love. Both
will live forever.

Bonnie had to bend down close to read the second,
smaller headstone.

Here lies Dominic McClelland, August 1946, adored
son of Matthew and Dulcie. Never was a child so
wanted or so loved. He only lived one short sweet hour
but will live in his mother's heart forever.

Bonnie's own heart almost burst with sadness as she
read those heart-wrenching inscriptions. The dates
showed that the child had been born only one month
after his father's death—possibly premature. Bad enough
to lose a husband, but one's only baby as well...

'You poor, poor woman,' Bonnie cried aloud.

She might have dissolved into tears again if the
presence which had guided her there had allowed it.
Instead, she found her gloominess replaced by an odd
burst of optimism.

Of course! she realised. The old lady had brought her
here to show her that, while she'd lost Jordan, she hadn't
lost his baby. She would at least have the child to hug
and hold and love. Their love-affair would never really
be over. It would live on in their offspring.

A second thought came to Bonnie, and, whirling, she
ran back to the house, racing into the kitchen to climb

up and bring down the baby-name book. Flipping over the pages, she found what she was looking for, gasping with discovery and delight. Dominic meant Sunday's child and her baby had been conceived on a Sunday! With a certainty that would not be denied she knew their baby was going to be a boy, and she was going to call him Dominic.

Hugging the book to her heart, Bonnie carried it up the stairs and into the nursery, half expecting to find the old lady's ghost sitting in the window-seat, waiting for her. And perhaps she was, only Bonnie could not see her.

Bonnie settled herself into that seat of dreams to dream a little herself, but as time passed her optimism gradually waned, the reality of her loneliness and lost love returning.

'I want to be brave,' she whispered aloud, both to the night sky and the old woman's presence. 'But don't you see? Jordan's gone, and I...I don't think I can live without him.'

This time there was no more supernatural sensations to comfort her. The room remained silent.

Maybe it had *always* been silent, she started thinking. Maybe the hopes and dreams, the fanciful romantic notions, had always been in her own imagination, no doubt inspired by this lonely old house with its lonely old owner, but created totally out of her own secret needs.

The moon drifted behind a cloud and Bonnie's face fell into darkness. She really should get up, go downstairs and turn on some lights. She had to go and lock the gates as well, Jordan having left them open.

It had to be getting late, she realised. At least nine. Time to face the real world again with its very real problems.

Keep thinking about the baby, she told herself. *Jordan's* baby. The baby would sustain her. It *had* to.

She sighed then turned to stand up, only to gasp at the sight of a dark shadow filling the doorway. The shadow moved immediately into the room, petrifying her till she saw who it was.

'Jordan!' she exclaimed, and collapsed back into the window-seat, shaken and shocked. 'You . . . you've come back.'

'Of course I've come back,' he ground out. 'I love you, even if you don't believe me.'

'I...I...' Bonnie clutched the baby book to her chest, staring up at him with wide eyes.

'I didn't leave because you told me to go. I left because I had to before I self-destructed with desire and despair.'

'Jordan, I——'

'No, don't interrupt, Bonnie,' he said, whirling to pace agitatedly around the nursery, his frustrated strides setting the cradle creaking. When he ground to a halt next to it, holding it firmly still in his hands and staring down into it, she almost died. Surely he didn't know? Surely he hadn't guessed?

But there was no knowledge of babies in his face when his eyes lifted. Only exasperation.

'I also knew that I could no longer go on trying to work out what were lies and what weren't. I knew you would never tell me the complete truth about yourself, so I decided to find out the facts for myself.'

'The facts?' she choked out.

'Yes, the facts. And I know now that your husband was the only other man you have ever been with. *I* am the only client you've ever slept with. And I . . . *I* am the only man you've ever loved, whether you're prepared to admit it or not!'

'How could you possibly know all that?' she gasped.

'I made it my business to find out.'

'*How*?'

'Firstly, I had a long chat with your boss.'

'Edgar?' she said weakly.

'The one and only. Direct man, that. I like him. He seemed to take to me a bit better when I told him how much I loved you. And then I spoke to Louise.'

'Louise?' Bonnie gasped. 'You spoke to Louise? But she...she's...'

'Cruising in the Pacific. Yes, so I found out from that delightful receptionist of yours, who, I might add, thinks you're the nicest lady she's ever met. Funny how often people told me the same story about you. Not a bad word to be found. Anyway, I rang Louise on the liner and we had a nice long chat.'

'Oh, God...'

'Well, you might start praying, you devious little twister of the truth. She was the one who told me your husband was your first lover, but that you had told her recently that you'd never really loved him. Louise then assured me that her sister would never *ever* go round sleeping with any man these days whom she didn't love to distraction. She told me convincingly that, having seen us together with her own eyes, you were crazy about me and if you pretended otherwise it was because you were afraid of being hurt again, afraid of putting your trust and your life in a man's hands. Was she right?'

'I...I...' The words just wouldn't come. They were there, on the tip of her tongue, but she was simply unable to say them. To say she loved him would not only be to put her own trust and life in his hands, but her baby's as well. Was she ready to do that? *Dared* she?

'Tell me to my face,' he said, striding over to lean against the window-frame, looming over her. 'Do you love me?'

Bonnie looked up, her heart bursting. How could she keep on denying her feelings? It was impossible. Come what may, she just had to tell him the truth.

'Yes,' she choked out. 'I...I've loved you all along.'

He groaned and yanked her up on to her feet, intent on kissing her. But when the book clanked to the floor between them he stopped to pick it up. 'What's this?'

The moonlight fell on to the title and he gasped before looking up with stunned eyes.

'A baby?' he rasped. 'You're having a baby? *We're* having a baby?'

She nodded, incapable of doing more.

'So when you said you couldn't get pregnant that day it...it was because you already *were*?'

Again, she nodded.

His cry was anguished. 'Oh, my darling, my beautiful, precious, foolish darling. You should have told me. You——' He broke off, placing the book in the cradle then turning to face her, his head shaking slowly from side to side. 'No...you did the right thing. It would have confused me even further at the time. Now I know what I want. To marry you and live in this house. To write books and raise a family. To live a simpler, far more fulfilling life.'

Bonnie could hardly believe what she was hearing. This was what she had dreamt about, what she had secretly hoped for. But it seemed too good to be true. He couldn't possibly mean to give up everything for her. He just couldn't!

'Are you sure, Jordan? Are you really sure?'

'I've never been surer in my whole life.'

'But what of your life in Sydney? Your career? Your ambition to become a judge?'

'That's not what I want any more. I don't think I ever really did. Frankly, when I was a boy, I wanted to be anything *but* a lawyer. I was always more like my mother, who was creative and sporty. But when I lost faith in her——'

He broke off, his face grimacing for a second before clearing to an expression of resignation. 'Look, you might as well know. I caught my mother with another man one afternoon when I was fifteen. I mean... right in the act, so to speak. It was a pretty dreadful shock. She tried to explain that she just couldn't help herself, that my father had been neglecting her for ages, but I wouldn't listen. All I saw was a devil where before she'd seemed a saint. I had no real concept of frustration and desire at that age. In my teenage boy's mind, she was nothing but a slut. I can see now I was a sanctimonious, judgemental little bastard.'

Bonnie felt sorry for him, but it explained a good deal about his earlier attitude to women and sex.

'From that day, I totally went my father's way,' he went on. 'I was determined not to be anything like my mother. Looking back, I can see that my fear of succumbing to any kind of uncontrollable sexual urges governed my private life. The women I dated tended to be on the cool, controlled side. Erica was basically as sexless as they come.'

'So you... you didn't go back to her after you left me that first time?'

'God, no. Look, I might as well confess fully. I was never engaged to her in the first place, though I was thinking about it.'

'But... but you said...'

'We both said a lot of things that weren't true, Bonnie. I also didn't make love to Erica that first week after meeting you. Oh, I admit I tried. I was desperate to forget you, desperate to believe that what I felt for you was nothing but frustration and could be cured with a night or two in another woman's bed. But as soon as I touched Erica all I could think about was green eyes and golden hair...'

His gaze went to those green eyes now, which were swimming with love for him.

'I only said I was engaged to her as a buffer against the appallingly weak feelings you were engendering in me. Feelings I've come to adore,' he murmured, putting the book down in the cradle and drawing her close. His kiss was long and lingering, and so full of true love that Bonnie wondered how she could ever have categorised Jordan's feelings as nothing but lust.

'What about your mother and father?' she asked him a little worriedly when their mouths finally parted. 'What will they say about all this? What will they think?'

'My father will worry and my mother will be proud of me.'

'But...'

'I had a long talk with my mother tonight too, when I went back to Sydney to get my things.'

'Yes?'

'She made me see what I have never seen before: that love is what matters in life above all else.'

'So you don't still loathe her?'

'No, I don't, though I do feel sorry for her. She really loves my father but they're an ill-matched pair. He'll never be capable of giving her the sort of love she needs. If she occasionally looks for the illusion of love elsewhere, who am I to judge?'

'I think I'm going to like your mother.'

'She already likes you, for making her son into a real man, not just a paper tiger.'

'You were always a real man, Jordan,' she praised, hugging him. 'Any man who did what you did today, stopping when you must have been aching to continue... I think that was wonderful. I think *you're* wonderful.'

'God, don't remind me. I didn't want to stop. I almost didn't.'

'But you did. That's all that matters. You did, whereas Richard wouldn't have.'

He jerked backwards to hold her at arm's length. 'Who the hell's Richard? I thought your husband's name was Keith?'

Bonnie blushed her guilt. 'I'm talking about Richard Halliday, the hero in your books.'

'*Hero*! That bloke's an out-and-out bastard! Hey, have you been sneaking around reading my books?'

'Only one.'

'Hmm. Methinks this needs further investigation. Which one?' He turned her round and they began walking together across the room.

'*The Trial of Norma Peacock.*'

'Ahh... my first.'

'It was good, Jordan. Very good. You're a wonderful writer.'

'Hmm. I like the sound of that. How wonderful?'

'How big is the ocean?'

Their laughter resounded all through the house.

Jordan stopped in the doorway and turned to the woman he loved more than life itself. 'Kiss me, Bonnie,' he said.

She did.

And if the lovers, locked in their embrace, had not been so oblivious of their surroundings, they might have heard a contented sigh ripple through the room behind them, or seen the pages of the book lying in the cradle flip over to the page on which the name Dominic was printed.

Never again would the cradle creak with a haunted breeze. Never again would it lie cold and empty and unused. The walls of the nursery would often echo with the sounds of laughter. A family had come to live in this once sad house. A family full of love. A family with a future.

The old woman's dream had finally come true.

EVER HAD ONE OF THOSE DAYS?

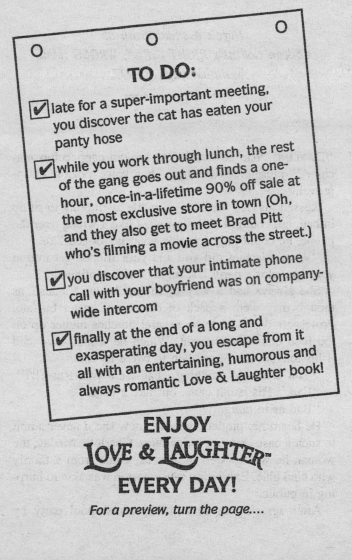

TO DO:

☑ late for a super-important meeting, you discover the cat has eaten your panty hose

☑ while you work through lunch, the rest of the gang goes out and finds a one-hour, once-in-a-lifetime 90% off sale at the most exclusive store in town (Oh, and they also get to meet Brad Pitt who's filming a movie across the street.)

☑ you discover that your intimate phone call with your boyfriend was on company-wide intercom

☑ finally at the end of a long and exasperating day, you escape from it all with an entertaining, humorous and always romantic Love & Laughter book!

ENJOY
LOVE & LAUGHTER™
EVERY DAY!

For a preview, turn the page....

"DARLING, YOU SOUND like a broken cappuccino machine," murmured Charlotte, her voice oozing disapproval.

Russell juggled the receiver while attempting to sit up in bed, but couldn't. If he *sounded* like a wreck over the phone, he could only imagine what he looked like.

"What mischief did you and your friends get into at your bachelor's party last night?" she continued.

She always had a way of saying "your friends" as though they were a pack of degenerate water buffalo. Professors deserved to be several notches higher up on the food chain, he thought. Which he would have said if his tongue wasn't swollen to twice its size.

"You didn't do anything...bad...did you, Russell?"

"Bad." His laugh came out like a bark.

"Bad as in *naughty*."

He heard her piqued tone but knew she'd never admit to such a base emotion as jealousy. Charlotte Maday, the woman he was to wed in a week, came from a family who bled blue. Exhibiting raw emotion was akin to burping in public.

After agreeing to be at her parents' pool party by

noon, he untangled himself from the bed sheets and stumbled to the bathroom.

"Pool party," he reminded himself. He'd put on his best front and accommodate Char's request. Make the family rounds, exchange a few pleasantries, play the role she liked best: the erudite, cultured English literature professor. After fulfilling his duties, he'd slink into some lawn chair, preferably one in the shade, and nurse his hangover.

He tossed back a few aspirin and splashed cold water on his face. Grappling for a towel, he squinted into the mirror.

Then he jerked upright and stared at his reflection, blinking back drops of water. "Good Lord. They stuck me in a wind tunnel."

His hair, usually neatly parted and combed, sprang from his head as though he'd been struck by lightning. "Can too many Wild Turkeys do that?" he asked himself as he stared with horror at his reflection.

Something caught his eye in the mirror. Russell's gaze dropped.

"What in the—"

Over his pectoral muscle was a small patch of white. A bandage. Gingerly, he pulled it off.

Underneath, on his skin, was not a wound but a small, neat drawing.

"A red heart?" His voice cracked on the word *heart*. Something—a word?—was scrawled across it.

"Good Lord," he croaked. "I got a tattoo. A heart tattoo with the name Liz on it."

Not Charlotte. Liz!

Let's Celebrate!

LOVE & LAUGHTER™

invites you to
the party of the season!

Grab your popcorn and be prepared to laugh as we celebrate with **LOVE & LAUGHTER**.

Harlequin's newest series is going Hollywood!

Let us make you laugh with three months of terrific books, authors and romance, plus a chance to win a FREE 15-copy video collection of the best romantic comedies ever made.

For more details look in the back pages of any Love & Laughter title, from July to September, at your favorite retail outlet.

Don't forget the popcorn!

Available wherever
Harlequin books are sold.

 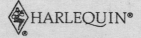 

◆ HARLEQUIN®

HARLEQUIN  PRESENTS®

Don't miss these fun-filled romances that feature
fantastic men who *eventually* make fabulous fathers.
Ready or not...

Watch for:
June 1997—FINN'S TWINS! (#1890)
by Anne McAllister
July 1997—THE DADDY DEAL (#1897)
by Kathleen O'Brien

FROM HERE TO PATERNITY—
men who find their way to fatherhood
by fair means, by foul, or even by default!

Available wherever Harlequin books are sold.

HARLEQUIN  PRESENTS®

Coming soon...